AF477095

THE LION IS RAMPANT

The scene is Britain in the 1980s, the economy in a malign spiral, with Westminster even more reliant upon the revenue from North Sea oil. In this crisis situation the Scottish Freedom Party infiltrates the major power centres and effectively controls events north of the Border.

After the takeover in Kenya, Nicholas Wainwright — a displaced white settler with a nose for adventure — comes to Scotland with hopes of setting up his own Highland cattle ranch. While reconnoitring likely territory, he stumbles on a plot of nightmarish global dimensions. By a draft agreement Scotland will leave NATO and receive military assistance from the USSR if Westminster decides to invade. A Soviet agent is already on hand: within days the document will be signed, making armed confrontation inevitable.

Calling on his own unaided resources, Wainwright steals a coded copy of the document and works his way south through the Cairngorms. He is hard pressed to escape the growing build-up of Republican forces in the Highlands. He is also uneasily aware of the sinister machinations of Maclean, the movement's ruthless arch-propagandist, by whose orders the Shetland Isles have just been 'pacified'.

This fast-paced narrative, vividly conveying the sensations of a merciless game of cat and mouse in the Highlands and Aberdeenshire, has a strong flavour of John Buchan. However, it is set against the kind of political developments in Scotland that Richard Hannay and his set could never have dreamed of.

THE LION IS RAMPANT

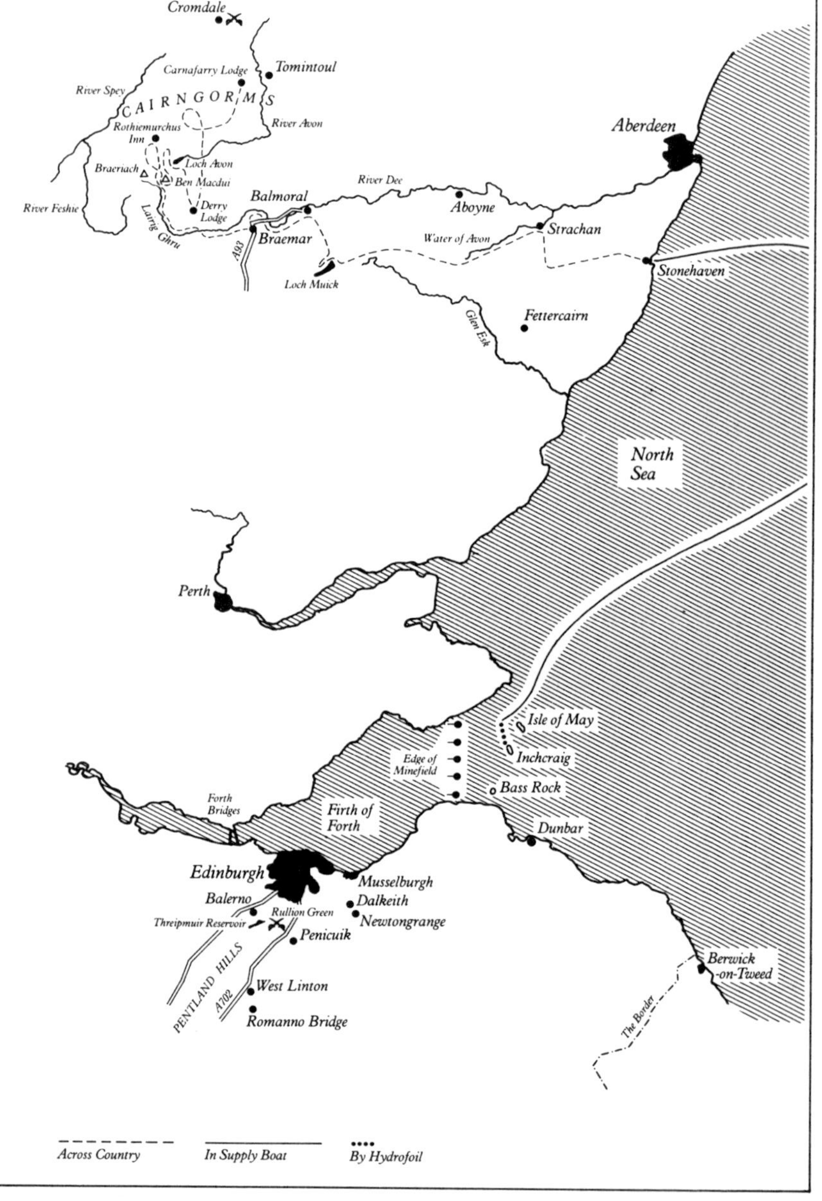

NICHOLAS WAINWRIGHT'S ESCAPE ROUTE
Cromdale
Tomintoul
Carnafarry Lodge
River Spey
CAIRNGORMS
River Avon
Rothiemurchus Inn
Aberdeen
Braeriach
Loch Avon
Ben Macdui
River Dee
River Feshie
Derry Lodge
Balmoral
Aboyne
Lairig Ghru
A93
Strachan
Braemar
Water of Avon
Stonehaven
Loch Muick
Glen Esk
Fettercairn
North Sea
Perth
Isle of May
Inchcraig
Edge of Minefield
Bass Rock
Forth Bridges
Firth of Forth
Dunbar
Edinburgh
Musselburgh
Balerno
Dalkeith
Rullion Green
Threipmuir Reservoir
Newtongrange
Penicuik
Berwick -on-Tweed
PENTLAND HILLS
A702
West Linton
The Border
Romanno Bridge
Across Country
In Supply Boat
By Hydrofoil

Ross Laidlaw

THE LION IS RAMPANT

THE MOLENDINAR PRESS
Glasgow

The Molendinar Press
73 Robertson Street,
Glasgow, Scotland

This edition first published 1979
© Ross Laidlaw
ISBN 0 904002 27 6

The characters and situations in *The Lion Is Rampant*
are entirely imaginary and bear no relation to any
real person or actual happening.

To Hermann and Malcolm

1

The Muzzled Lion

MY PULSES QUICKENED as I turned into Princes Street. Across the gardens the silhouette of Edinburgh's Old Town towered against the sky in a breathtaking fretwork of spires, domes and turrets, leading up to the castle perched on its rock four hundred feet above my head.

I am no lover of cities, having spent most of my life in the African bush, but I had to admit there was something about Edinburgh that stirred the blood. Being built on different levels, like the galleries of a tropical rain forest, may have had something to do with it. From bridges spanning stone valleys, fantastic glimpses were caught of other Edinburghs far below — an encapsulated village or an ancient, rotting slum. Here and there grassy summits, with woods, lochs, wildfowl and grazing sheep, were thrust like surrealistic islands above the rooftops.

The bright, tingling April weather put me in mind of the Kenya Highlands where I'd run my father's farm since his death five years ago, resigning my commission to do so. Then late last year, only a few years after Kenyatta's death, a dreary Maoist-style regime came to power, and my farm had been taken over as a collective by the Kenya People's Republic.

So here I was, Old Africa Hand, making a new start in strange terrain. I took stock as I strode along. Thirty-five, single, and in hard physical shape. Background: Prince of Wales School, Nairobi, a majority in the Kenya Army, then several years' farming experience.

Leaving Princes Street, I struck north into the Georgian magnificence of the New Town (incredibly solid and splendid for eyes accustomed to tin-roofed bungalows and thatched native huts) and headed for McKendrick's where I'd arranged to meet Rachel. A notice beside a news-stand brought me up short — SACK GRIMBLE DEMANDS CHAMBER.

I found the British political situation baffling and had just about given up trying to understand it by following the media. But this notice somehow had a smell of urgency to it. Somewhat reluctantly I bought the rag.

I had reached the steps leading down from the pavement to McKendrick's. To describe the place as a self-service basement restaurant would be rather like dismissing Chaka as just another Zulu guerilla. For McKendrick's had a significance vastly exceeding its function to purvey salad meals and coffee. It considered itself the nerve-centre of an articulate and influential (and to my mind rather odious) subculture continuously discussing The New Scotland. The place was always crammed to the gunwales with writers in jeans and fishermen's jerseys, professional negroes in close-fitting polo necks making a big production of being black and beautiful, outlandish figures in Castro beards and kepis, cranks who wrote and talked the Verra Tung — an uncouth gibberish which, its adherents claimed, was the pure medieval Scots before dilution and anglicisation set in — and other hangers-on in combat jackets and second-hand evening trousers: the ubiquitous uniform of youth.

I detested the place wholeheartedly. Its patrons seemed to me, without exception, to be arrogant and opinionated. The only reason I ever went there was to squire Rachel, a fellow Kenyan who represented an African news agency and who liked to 'be in touch with the heather roots', as she put it. Keeping her ear to the ground to pick up current trends was important in her line of business. To watch her in action at McKendrick's — feelers out picking up vibrations, talking and arguing forcibly with a quicksilver brilliance — was almost compensation enough for the irritation which the place induced in me.

A solid blast of noise roared out as I opened the door. I fought my way to the end of the queue, squeezing between the wooden railings and the food stands crammed with vegetarian salads. Notices on the walls proclaimed the virtues of Cassava Couscous ... Yams with Plantain a la Dahomey ("a gastronomic experience you'll never forget") ... Palmkernel Kebab ... and today's speciality — Seaweed Pudding ("guaranteed ethnic and organic"). Not an honest chip or sausage in sight.

"Dandelion?" enquired the counter-girl brightly, when I asked for coffee.

"No — just plain, ordinary bean." It made me feel as if I had asked for a double Scotch at a temperance meeting. By the time I had barged a passage to a table, my hackles were beginning to bristle. In my tie and lightweight suit I felt out of place. Even my longish hair, I decided, probably looked like a crude and hastily-donned disguise, resembling the macs and trilbies once worn by plain clothes policemen in an attempt to blend in with the crowd.

I stirred my coffee moodily, feeling out of my element and somewhat disorientated, not just in the exotic setting of McKendrick's but with regard to the whole experience of trying to adjust to life in Britain. In Africa circumstances are often trying, sometimes cataclysmic — a bush fire, a swarm of locusts, a political coup. Coping with them, however, is usually a straightforward business — you either win out or you have to pack in. But in Britain there seemed to be no clear-cut answers to any issue, no effective solutions to problems like strikes, vandalism, or an ailing economy. And the suggested remedies of many leading politicians were, to my way of thinking, too often impractical, last-ditch gimmickry.

I looked round the crowded restaurant. Everyone seemed to be shouting at everybody else, faces thrust out intently, hands chopping and waving as if practising karate or some modern type of ballet. There was very little genuine laughter — these people took their opinions much too seriously for that. A bearded youth in baggy silk pantaloons, carrying a tray and talking over his shoulder at someone, barged against my table, slopping some of my hard-won coffee.

"Steady on," I growled, glaring at him.

"Sor-ry," he said, raising his eyebrows as a cultured Roman might have done on finding a stray Goth in his bathwater.

At the table next to mine a man with a half-familiar face rather like a revitalised skull was holding forth to a crowd of young men, with a girl or two among them, all sporting Fiery Cross badges. Every day you saw more and more of these Cran Tara regalia. They seemed to be mostly worn by students, lecturers, executives, ad-men, planners — the intellectual and business spearhead of the newly-formed Scottish Freedom Party.

Suddenly I remembered where I'd seen Skull-Face — on TV recently, ranting on about the need for total separation from England. Maclean —that was his name. At the time I remember I'd put him down as a dangerous fanatic and something more. He had emanated a quality of what I can only describe as unhealthy spleen that was quite frightening. Separation from the tyrannous English for Maclean was no mere economic or political issue. It was a crusade, for the success of which any extremes of violence or bloodshed would seem to be justified. I had already seen more than enough of this during my African upbringing.

I glanced at my paper and the headlines leapt out at me — CHAMBER CHALLENGES WESTMINSTER. I scanned the columns:"...Whitehall's decision to scrap the Aukness Bridge.... storm breaks in the Chamber... last word over The Brig should rest with the Scottish Development Agency not Whitehall, maintains Tam Linn, leader of the Scottish Freedom Party, whose suggestion that the Minister for Internal Relations should resign was met with cheers and shouts of approval throughout the Chamber by members of the SNP and Freedom Party alike... "

The rest of the front page was standard stuff — layoffs, closures, picketings etc., so I leafed through the pages to the editorial on the Chamber row. It was headed "Aukness — an Industrial Rubicon?"

The Readers Letters page was full of furious protests against the axing of the Aukness Project. Especially vehement was one written over the name of a prominent Nationalist MP:

"... a classic example of the incompetence and insensitivity we have come to expect from Westminster in her dealings with Scotland... pledged her financial backing for one of the most daring engineering projects of our time... would have triggered the development of a communications network of inestimable importance to the infrastructure of North Sea Oil... increased expenditure which was more than balanced by the proceeds of the trail-blazing ScotLot... produced brilliant solutions to staggering technical problems — the construction of a special harbour to allow raw materials to be brought in, the conveying of huge pre-fabricated steel sections to the site, the sway factor affecting the enormously tall uprights which the vast distance to be spanned necessitated, combatted by the hair-raising business of spinning the massive cables over the uprights to guy them down... endless labour problems arising from difficulties in driving concrete piles and excavating cable anchorages... a symbol of Scotland's confidence in herself and in her engineering expertise, and a source of pride to Scots everywhere... The withdrawal of funds promised to the Scottish Development Agency is not only an act of cowardly and unprincipled duplicity, but a shameful betrayal of Scotland's interests, a betrayal to which those stark, unfinished uprights, towering above the water at Aukness, bear mute yet eloquent testimony."

Resentfully, I dropped the paper onto the seat beside me. I'd had a bellyful of political improvement back in Kenya and would have given a lot to have been spared any more. But with the rest of the UK fast disappearing under a loathsome scab of industrial development, I couldn't have settled happily anywhere else in Britain except Scotland, where a man could at least still get a lungful of wholesome air. Next week I was seeing a chap at the Land Use Development Board about my idea of starting a cattle ranch in the Highlands. If that came off I would be a happy man. I'd be living the kind of life I enjoyed; also I reckoned that in the great open spaces of the North I should be able to find my personal bearings.

At the table next to me the man Maclean was beginning to get into his stride. I listened, idly at first, then with quickening interest.

"Scotland is being bled white," he was expounding, in his soft West Highland voice, to a rapt audience. "Every week Westminster closes down more of our factories, another shipyard, axes one more of the few railways still left to us, holds back funds promised to the Chamber. The Chamber of Scotland," Maclean sneered contemptuously, " — a paper parliament with less teeth than a District Sewage Committee. A worthless sop to appease Scotland's demand for nationhood. When we complain, does Westminster listen? Does it think with shame and concern of the growing dole queues in Scotland's cities, of mothers going without so that their bairns shall not be hungry? No — the only answer we get from Westminster is yet another cant slogan about 'tightening our belts' or 'all pulling together'." He looked round the circle of intent young faces surrounding him and his eyes glittered. "I tell you, that Scotland's only hope for the future is to cut free from England. Not partnership, not devolution, not some half-baked federal compromise, but separation — complete, irrevocable. Remember 79! The English in Westminster killed the Assembly even though the greatest number of votes were cast in favour of it in Scotland. That was just the start of their campaign to stamp out every vestige of independence and make Scotland a mere province of England. What has Scotland ever gained from England that she should wish to preserve a partnership which has drained away her wealth, her brains and the flower of her sons? What has been the cause of all Scotland's ills since the year seventeen hundred and seven and before? What is it that has prevented Scotland from becoming a free and wealthy nation? I look round at you, my young eagles, and I see the answer in your faces. Our bondage to the English — that is the cancer that is eating away our nation's life. Am I not right?"

A growl of assent swirled round the circle. Quite a crowd was gathering around the table on all sides, hemming me in.

"Must this always be so?" Maclean went on, his voice dropping almost to a whisper. "Must we endure the English yoke for ever?" He paused dramatically, then went on in a voice that rose almost to a shout. "I say 'No More' I say the time has come to break the chains that bind us, to cast out the viper from our midst. The English seek, as they have always done, to lull our doubts with smooth words: Our Industry, our Commerce, all the organs of our national life are filled with Englishry, deadening our will, sapping our power. Let us root them out. Half Scotland is owned by wealthy English living lives of pampered ease furth of the Border, from the sweat of their Scottish tenants. What do these parasites contribute to Scotland? Nothing. Let us restore the land to its rightful owners. When the last Englishman leaves Scotland, when the last tie with Westminster is broken, then and only then will Scotland be free."

I decided that I couldn't listen to any more of this insidious claptrap and keep silent. Maclean, with his rhetoric and powerful personality, had gained an ascendancy over these youngsters and was corrupting their minds. It was just this sort of propaganda which, once it had gained a hold, had brought about the ruin of my own country, Kenya. And it had been much the same story with Amin's Uganda.

I chose my moment carefully, just when Maclean was at his most malevolent, speaking almost in a whisper.

"I've never heard such poisonous rot in all my life," I said loudly.

Faces turned and stared at me, whilst a silence spread throughout McKendrick's rather as ripples extend from where a stone is dropped into a pool. I hadn't really thought just what effect my words would produce and I suddenly felt self-conscious and uncomfortable. However I couldn't withdraw now.

Maclean turned slowly and studied me, eyes glittering, head cocked to one side appraisingly. I thought of a deadly snake in the bush poised to strike.

"Oh?" he rejoined in the softest, blandest tone imaginable. "Perhaps you would be kind enough to explain why you think so. We would be very interested to hear your reasons."

"I don't know enough facts and figures to take you up on your claim that Scotland's lost out on being a partner with England," I plunged, feeling rather like a bull in the ring. "Although I should imagine there's another side to the argument which it suits your book to ignore. What really sickens me is the way you seem prepared to stir up emotions at their lowest level. Appealing to instincts of fear and greed to achieve your ends."

"Oh, fear and greed is it?" Maclean sounded as if he were reading aloud from some choice wine list. He grinned at me. "I wonder now if that doesn't have the merest hint, just a teeny, weeny suspicion of, ah —the pot calling the kettle black? To use an English expression."

A delighted buzz from Maclean's followers greeted this sally. I felt palpable hostility building up against me.

"You all look decent young chaps to me," I went on, switching my address to Maclean's circle of devotees. "Can't you see that he's using you, that you're just pawns in whatever game it is he's playing? I know —I've seen his type in action in Africa. And experienced the results. If you think that freedom of speech, toleration, the rights of the individual are just so much out-of-date lumber, well, go right ahead and swallow what he's serving up to you. Then you'll all become good little totalitarians in no time."

"Ay say — theah's a wather bad smell in heah," said another youth, parodying a cultured English accent and holding his nose. My own accent is, for want of a better term, standard English: unlike the clipped twang of the South African or Zimbabwian white there is no detectable Kenya accent among settlers of English descent. I felt the mood of Maclean's coterie begin to change from sullen resentment to a schoolboyish glee in finding a victim to bait.

Some of the youths began to snigger and ominous mutters broke out: "Bad smells belong tae the stank... chuck the Sassenach oot... let's gie him a lesson he'll no forget..."

This was turning ugly. I didn't want trouble, but if any of them laid a hand on me they could end up getting hurt, for I knew I wouldn't be able to stop myself from lamming out. Though I say it myself, I'm pretty handy in a scrap; even though in this case the odds were rather daunting and not an ally in sight.

And then Rachel arrived.

She made quite an entrance. Rachel always had style and presence, and that morning her black skin created a stunning effect against the cream suit and accessories she was wearing. She swept through McKendrick's, waving and calling to acquaintances although, I suspect, immediately aware of the tension.

"Hello, Nick, sorry I'm late," she announced, then turned and treated Maclean to a brilliant, glacial smile. "Hope I'm not breaking anything up."

Maclean gave one of his death's-head leers. "Och, not at all, not at all, lassie," he purred equably. "We had just finished a very interesting wee crack." He turned to his followers who had suddenly become transmuted into a gaggle of awkward schoolboys. "Come on lads, we have work to do in the Grassmarket, remember?" And with a final look in my direction which I won't forget in a hurry he stalked out followed by his troop.

As the door of McKendrick's closed behind them, talk burst out again throughout the restaurant, as though someone had turned on a tap. I realised I was soaked with sweat and shaking slightly.

"Lucky you've got big sister Rachel to look after you," she said sternly. I had only known her a few weeks — like myself she was a Kenyan expatriate and it sometimes felt as if we had shared the same childhood. "You don't want to tangle with Maclean, Nick. He's way out of your league."

"As I was beginning to find out," I observed ruefully. "Thanks for cooling the situation. I had the feeling that Maclean had only to snap his fingers and his dogs would have gone for me in a pack. Where are they off to now?"

"They're hanging an effigy of the Minister for Internal Relations as a protest over this latest Westminster decision on the Bridge. Just a publicity stunt, but it's effective. Maclean's an extremely skilful demagogue. He's not like the average politico who's more interested in preserving his image than in advancing the policies he's supposed to stand for. Maclean's your genuine, 22-carat, hallmarked fanatic. There's nothing he wouldn't stop at to advance The Cause — he's a sort of propaganda agent for Tam Linn's Freedom Party. He doesn't scare, and safeguarding his reputation is the last thing he'd worry about."

"Who *is* this Tam Linn I keep hearing about?"

"Nick, don't you have eyes or ears? I'll give you the media profile. Born and bred in the slums and pulled himself up by his bootstraps. Broke off a brilliant career at University to take up social work and politics —some of his work with down-and-outs and youngsters, in poor areas, was pretty terrific. Then became the rising young star of SNP — until last year, when he pulled out and formed his own show — the Scottish Freedom Party. The SNP weren't prepared to be radical enough for him over the issue of securing independence."

"Suggesting that the Freedom Party's prepared to use force?"
"Well, they haven't actually spelled it out yet. Now let's stop talking politics, Nick. All this excitement has made me hungry. For rescuing you from Maclean's tartan hordes you can fetch me a huge Cuban rice salad. With paw-paws and spiced aubergines."
The way she said it almost convinced me it might be appetising.

2
The Lion Roars

THE OFFICES of the Land Use Development Board are in a stately Georgian house in Edinburgh's New Town. I was shown into a large, pleasant room with an Adam fireplace and a ceiling of fine plasterwork.

A thick-set elderly man was standing on the hearthrug. He strode towards me and shook my hand in a firm and vigorous grip. He had the face of an Old Testament prophet and a splendid head of silver hair.

"Pringle," he introduced himself. "Sit ye down, laddie." He waved me into an armchair. I smiled inwardly: no-one had called me 'laddie' for close on twenty years. "I'll stand if ye don't mind. Never could learn the trick o' sitting still. I see frae yere application that yere name's Nicholas Wainwright." He shot me a keen glance from under bushy eyebrows. "Ye'll be Ned Wainwright's boy. Same yellow thatch, same eyes — ane blue, the ither grey. I kenned your father thirty years ago in Kenya, when I grew pyrethrum up Thomson's Falls way. He was a guid man, was Ned."

Pringle filled and lit a battered briar, then, trailing wreaths of blue smoke, began to perambulate up and down before the hearthrug.

"Well, Nicholas — ye'll no mind me calling ye Nicholas — I'm afraid I've got bad news for ye. No more Land Grants for an indefinite period." He pointed to a manilla envelope on the mantelpiece. "Orders frae Whitehall."

"But — I thought the Land Board was financed by the Scottish Development Agency!"

"Aye — and so it should be," growled Pringle. "But those damned meddlin' eediots in Westminster have cut back the Agency's funds at source. Which they've nae right to do. Part o' their national economy drive. If only they'd let Scotland run her ain affairs, we'd be a sight better off."

"Converting peat-bog and grouse moor into productive land — surely that's a sound investment for the future."

"Of course it is!" exploded Pringle, wheeling round at the end of his circuit and stabbing his pipe-stem at me for emphasis. "It's been estimated that in ten or twelve years any money invested in Land Grants would have multiplied at least fourfold from the sale o' produce. Only thae blind, penny-pinching Whitehall Johnnies cannae or willnae see it. Man, it fairly makes your blood boil. But Tam Linn'll make it hot for them. He's campaignin' for Grimble tae come and answer tae the Chamber for Westminster's policy."

"Tam Linn — he's for total separation, isn't he?"

"Can ye blame him?" retorted Pringle fiercely. "He's a grand lad is oor Tam. And he's got Scotland behind him. The Freedom Pairty's sweepin' up seats wi' every local and by-election. The Labour men and the Nationalists had better look tae their laurels. It's my jalouse the Freedom Pairty'll take over frae them at the elections in May. And a guid thing for Scotland tae. I shouldn't be saying this to ye, mind."

Next morning I took myself off to the Pentlands to try and forget my disappointment in a bout of stiff hiking. On the slopes of Wether Law, with glorious springy turf beneath my feet and wholesome hill air filling my lungs, I could almost imagine myself back in my native Aberdares; the oppressive atmosphere of political tension which loomed so large in the capital fell into perspective. I felt at peace for the first time in days when I came down off the hill at Carlops. While waiting in a grand old coaching inn for the bus back into town, I drank beer with herds and hill-farmers — decent kindly folk whose talk of cattle prices and black-faced 'yowes' was music to my ears. Land Grant or no Land Grant, I determined not to give up my plans to start a stock-farm.

It was a mild, sunny afternoon when I got off the bus and set out across the Meadows for my flat. Half way there my attention was caught by the sight of a large crowd surrounding a speaker on a platform. Even at a distance there was something about the stance and the tone of voice that was arresting. I drifted over to listen. Asking who the speaker was, I was told 'Tam Linn'.

Before I had reached the outskirts of the crowd I was aware of the man's charisma. In part this was sheer physical presence — six foot three or four with flaming red hair and beard, a great cliff of brow and compelling eyes. The content of his speech was straightforward enough

— a statement of the need for total commitment by the Scottish people to the cause of gaining from Whitehall powers for the Chamber that would make it truly the voice of Scotland. Clear, direct and forceful as his actual words were, it was his ability to get alongside his audience and to carry them with him that impressed me most, a gift possessed to any great degree by only one other man that I have heard — old Jomo Kenyatta. It wasn't just masterly rhetoric either. Tam Linn's sincerity was manifest with every word he spoke.

I was so caught up with his words that it was quite a time before I noticed standing beside the rostrum none other than Maclean, with a barrel-chested young thug in tow. The sight of that cadaverous figure made my nerves tingle involuntarily. There was something hypnotically sinister about Maclean: the man seemed to radiate evil in an almost physical way. My brush with him at McKendrick's, albeit slight, had given me a hint of his force and single-mindedness — attributes which if misdirected could, in Maclean's case I felt sure, wreak incalculable harm.

"Wha will be a coward knave?" Tam Linn concluded, evidently quoting from a poem familiar to his audience. He stared with blazing eyes above the heads of his listeners, one arm uplifted. With most speakers this would have been a dangerous way to end — over-dramatic and corny. But with him it was somehow exactly right. You could feel the determination and sense of solidarity that his words had stirred up in his hearers.

The crowd broke up in almost total silence, a look of grim determination in nearly every face that contrasted starkly with the complacency of the faithful at most political Jamborees.

Another facet of this strange man was revealed to me a few days later when I noticed in a bookshop a slim volume entitled *Liberty's in Every Blow.* "As though Robert Burns had collaborated with William Dunbar," said the blurb inside the dust-cover. I glanced through the book. I don't pretend to know much about poetry but some of the pieces it contained gripped me. They seemed charged with a rugged strength, humanity and passionate love of country.

Meanwhile, spray-painted graffiti everywhere reflected the rising discontent as relations between Westminster and Edinburgh continued to deteriorate: "Assembly Yes — Chamber No" — "It's Scotland's Oil" — "Hands off Aukness" — "We gar'd them rin at Bannockburn" (a song by The Gomerils, Scotland's leading folk group) — "Save the Braemars", crude metaphors about chamber pots and more in the same vein. When the Braemars, Scotland's oldest and best-loved regiment, were finally disbanded, public indignation reached a peak. Stand Firm — the regiment's motto — was taken up throughout Scotland as the slogan of a new spirit of resolution and defiance.

One evening soon afterwards I had a phone call from Rachel.

"Nick — the Minister has agreed to come to Edinburgh for a summit meeting with the Chamber." She sounded excited.

"Oh yes?" For politeness' sake I tried to project some enthusiasm.

"Seems Tam Linn and Co have been putting the screws on him. They're going to raise Cain over Aukness and some of the other economic cut-backs. The whole business of Ultimate Powers is to be thrashed out. And they want extensive coverage from me. They're going to give it lead story position in the bulletins."

"Hey — that's great. Congratulations."

"I'm allowed to take a friend into the Press Gallery. I'll see the Secretary of the Lobby and get a card for you." There was a short pause and she went on, rather sharply, "Nick — you're not saying anything. I take it you'd like to come?"

"Wouldn't miss it for worlds," I lied gallantly.

A few mornings later, in early May, we drove to the Chamber Buildings — an imposing pile which looked as if it had been hijacked from the Acropolis. The place was humming with police and security guards but our press cards ensured that we got in without fuss.

We made out way into a large chamber, in the middle of which concentric tiers of seats descended to an oval, railed-off space like the arena in a Roman amphitheatre. The chamber was lighted by three large windows at the north end. Two galleries on pillars ran the lengths of the eastern and western walls.

We were ushered upstairs to one of the galleries which was already half-full of reporters. The scene at our feet had an unreal quality. Here, where it had been planned in the late 70s that a Scottish Assembly should meet, its ghost was now convening. To my eyes it seemed very much a puppet parliament, mimicking the motions of constitutional power but without any real significance. It reminded me of Roman History lessons and tales of the powerlessness of the Senate against the later emperors.

The tiers below us were beginning to fill with Chamber members, dark-suited for the most part but with here and there a kilt to give a splash of colour. I spotted Tam Linn by his fiery hair and beard. There was some waving and calling of greetings then silence spread throughout the great chamber as Sir Archibald Grimble and his men took their seats. All stood for prayers after which the Chairman of the Chamber made a short introductory speech in which he stated in a flat, dispassionate voice that the Chamber was dissatisfied firstly with Westminster's handling of certain economic affairs as they applied to Scotland, and secondly with the whole question of Westminster's Ultimate Prerogative and in particular with the influence exercised by the Minister for Internal Relations in regard to the Aukness Project. In response to a request by the Chamber, the Minister had agreed to make a full statement concerning Westminster's policy in these areas and to hear the views of the Chamber. The Chairman then called upon Sir Archibald Grimble to speak.

I craned my neck over the gallery railing to get a better view of 'the Hammer of the Scots' as the Minister rose to his feet. Grimble was a bulky man of medium height, dressed in one of those pale, dove-coloured, double-breasted suits beloved of top American executives. His face, matching his suit in its pallor, was calm and composed, with harsh lines running from the eagle nose to the corners of the thin, lawyer's mouth. Above the heavy-lidded eyes rose a domed head — befitting a man of iron will and cold, logical mind, I thought. He immediately put me in mind of a great bird of prey.

"The Scottish Chamber have asked me here," he began, speaking in a harsh, weary-sounding voice, "to answer on behalf of the sovereign government of Westminster, certain charges which the subordinate Chamber has preferred against the said government." He paused while his hooded eyes moved round the crowded tiers. "I use the words 'sovereign' and 'subordinate' deliberately, Mr. Chairman. For let us not mince our words. The issues which we are here assembled to discuss are too portentous to allow of any glossing over of unwelcome or unpleasant realities. The matters referred to are ones with fundamental implications for our *British* Constitution." Once more his basilisk gaze swept slowly round the tense audience, allowing time for that charged word to sink in. "First, and possibly most important, because though hardly different in kind to, it is greater in degree than, the other — ah, grievances, listed by the Chamber, is the business of Aukness."

A muted sigh and stir, like wind in a cornfield, rippled round the tiers.

"I am not unaware, Mr. Chairman, of the fact that the postponement of the Aukness project represents the loss of many thousands of jobs. At a time of economic recession and widespread unemployment this may have seemed a short-sighted move."

Grimble was here interrupted by sarcastic cries of "complete bloody blindness!" and "try telling it to Westminster!" Several members rose with the evident intention of taking him up.

"No — I will not give way at this point," continued the Minister, "in order to counter arguments which I suspect are based on emotion rather than on reasoned appraisal of the facts. To continue — it has been said, with some degree of truth, that politics represents the triumph of the urgent over the important. No one will be able to hold me guilty of this charge regarding my advice to Westminster concerning Aukness. All you ladies and gentlemen of the Chamber must know that never at any stage in the planning of decentralisation of certain Scottish businesses to Edinburgh was there any question of a separate economy based on local resources. It is the considered view of the government in Westminster that Aukness, if allowed to go ahead, would saddle the country with a crippling load of expense which it would be folly to incur at this moment."

From all over the benches members leapt to their feet and for at least a minute there was uproar. The Chairman repeatedly called for order, and at last quiet was restored.

"I fear I must repeat myself by insisting that I will not give way to interruptions at this point," Grimble went on, in the tones of a stern schoolmaster reproving an unruly class. "I shall however enlarge on a remark made by one of the vociferous gentlemen. I refer to the powers of the Scottish Development Agency relative to those of Westminster. Let me quote from the Statute Book: 'The United Kingdom economy will always be managed as *one* unit... The UK Parliament will remain absolutely sovereign in *all* matters, whether decentralised or not... The Government in Westminster will hold complete and final authority to sanction or dismiss any proposed executive action by the Chamber! I could go on, Mr. Chairman, but that should suffice to make it clear beyond any possible doubt that there is no question whatever that Westminster exceeded her authority regarding the decision about Aukness."

"In other words, Westminster can manipulate the Chamber in any way it likes," called out one kilted member from the Freedom Party benches. "In the last resort the Chamber has no final say. Is that it?"

"The Member is incontrovertibly out of order in interrupting.

However, I shall comment on the point he raises. The final say does indeed lie with Westminster. And for the very good reason that without such power reserved to Westminster, there would be no ultimate safeguard against the breaking up of the Kingdom. Let me quote again: 'The Unity of the United Kingdom must be preserved — to the benefit of all our citizens.'"

A chorus of groans rose from the Nationalist and Freedom Party benches in response to what was evidently an over-familiar and unpopular catch-phrase.

"You may groan, gentlemen, but I would ask you to consider objectively, what results would stem from a too-powerful Chamber in Scotland."

"We'd get rid of the Minister for Internal Relations for a start," shouted the member for Easter Ross. "Aye — and demand the return of the Secretary of State for Scotland", called out another voice.

Grimble continued unperturbed. "Let me enumerate the certain ill-consequences that would follow from having such a Chamber. Firstly, there would be an increasing demand for Scotland to have the lion's share of revenues accruing from North Sea oil."

Grimble paused to allow his *mot juste* to be appreciated, but once again the member for Easter Ross broke in, spoiling the effect.

"Well, why not? It's our oil."

"I see," continued Grimble smoothly. "But if we accept the worthy gentleman's arguments, we would have to concede that County Durham had a right to her own coal, that Cornwall could export her Kaolin to Japan instead of to the Potteries, and so on. Perhaps the worthy gentleman envisages a state of affairs in which Lancashire draws up trading agreements with Yorkshire."

If Grimble had expected this sally to raise a laugh, he was to be disappointed: apart from a mild Unionist titter the Chamber maintained a sullen silence.

"We must be very clear in this matter Mr. Chairman," Grimble went on. "It is *not* Scotland's Oil. To pretend otherwise is to indulge not only in self-deception but to allow selfishness and greed to determine our political thinking. To admit Scotland's right to exploit the oil deposits of the North Sea for herself would be to give a signal for the general break-up of our nationalised industries, which would result in the loss of our present system of cross-subsidisation and would lead inevitably to the destruction of the economic unity of the United Kingdom. I repeat, control of regional and industrial policies together with the destination of oil revenues must remain the ultimate responsibility of Westminster. Any other arrangement must lead irrevocably towards the downhill path to separation. To say that this would not follow, would be hypocrisy of the most —"

"What's wrong with separation? Are we to be considered less responsible than a self-governing member of the Commonwealth?" Another interruption from Tam Linn's section of the hall.

"If the worthy gentleman really thinks *that* then I fear he is deceiving himself. Independence is a sure recipe for poverty."

At this a babel of voices broke out and order had again to be restored.

"Oh, yes. Consider the facts." Grimble proceeded to reel off statistics about identifiable public expenditure, comparison of English and Scottish unemployment rates and earnings and estimates about Scotland's balance of trade, each one greeted with challenges and angry expostulations. But Grimble swept on with his list, propping up his statistics with an elaborate buttressing of facts and figures which sounded convincing enough but which I suspected probably didn't amount to conclusive proof. Brushing aside further interruptions, he went on to defend in detail Westminster's policy concerning the economic cut-backs to which the Chamber had raised objection, and concluded with a re-statement of the ultimate sovereignty of the Westminster Parliament. He sat down amid a hostile silence from the Nationalist and Freedom Party benches and a few scattered cheers from other parts of the Chamber.

In the continuing debate the burden of the Nationalist argument was a rejection of the Minister's power to influence Westminster by terms of his Monitorial Commission, anger over the distress in Scotland caused by Westminster's economic policies, dissatisfaction with the machinery of granting funds and a demand for full Chamber control of the Scottish Development Agency together with much greater powers in the fields of economy and industry. Grimble agreed to put all these points before the Westminster Parliament but made it clear that he was personally opposed to them and would speak out against them at Westminster. To my surprise there was almost as much heckling of these speakers by the small but vocal band of Freedom Party Members around Tam Linn. From where I sat I could see one profile of their leader, and he never uttered a word.

At one o'clock, the Chamber adjourned for lunch. My ticket didn't allow me to join Rachel and the other journalists in the bar so I wandered about Calton Hill, as it was a fine summery day with a pleasant breeze, munching my sandwiches and looking at the weirdly-assorted monuments. At my feet Edinburgh unrolled itself, the Gothic fantasy of the Old Town confronting the ordered geometry of the New across the great divide of Princes Street and the gardens. High above the tallest spires, the castle loomed in brooding magnificence, the grim semi-circle of her Half-Moon Bastion frowning down upon the city below. In such a scene of peace and beauty it seemed that time had stopped and history was openly displayed in a glass case.

I returned to the Chamber to find the place buzzing with expectancy. Tam Linn was to speak next.

A tense hush spread as the last members filed into the tiers. Then Tam Linn, Leader of the Scottish Freedom Party and member for Granton and Leith, rose to speak — a dominating figure with his height, his flaming mane of hair and eyes that glowed darkly from under that lofty forehead. Once again, as when I had first heard him speak in the Meadows, I felt the power of the man's feelings. The restraint imposed upon him to put those feelings in lucid speech only made the effect of his words more powerful.

"Well, gentlemen," he began, in a moderate tone of voice — resonant and slightly guttural. "We have now heard the Minister's answer to the charges made by the Scottish Chamber against the English Parliament in Westminster. We have heard these charges pressed home with considerable force and logic by various members sitting in this Chamber. And we have heard the message which the Minister will take back to his masters in Westminster. What is that message? A preparedness to reconsider the savage economic strictures which have brought such widespread misery and unemployment to Scotland? A promise that the Chamber's just and reasonable request for an extension of her powers be at least given appraisal by Westminster? No — we have been given a flat refusal, arrogant, unyielding, final. The Minister has shown us only too clearly that both he and the English Parliament hold the idea of Scottish nationhood in contempt. We now know what this Chamber can expect from Westminster. As far as London is concerned we must remain content with the shadow of power, grateful for whatever political crumbs are dropped from Westminster's table, while the substance resides with an alien government south of the Border. We have seen the manifest hypocrisy of that government in first of all granting to the Scottish Development Agency executive powers, only to rescind these powers when it disagrees with the Chamber's plans as in the case of Aukness. An economic eunuch is what this Chamber is to become, if Westminster has its way. Take heed, for the knife is already brandished and once the deed is done our manhood is lost for ever.

"The Minister would have us believe that a fully independent Scotland would be doomed to poverty. We in Scotland have heard this argument time and again during the two hundred and eighty years that have elapsed since the Union, and we have grown weary of it. It is an argument based on jealousy and fear. For make no mistake — England has always stood to gain at the expense of Scotland in this unequal partnership. And now, after nearly three centuries of exploitation, Westminster dares to accuse us of selfishness and greed when we talk of Scotland's oil. They know, very well indeed, that a separate Scotland would be a strong, rich country. Even certain parties who feel more loyalty to international socialism than their own country have admitted that secession would deal a 'shattering blow' to the English economy.

What are the facts? Scotland is self-supporting in food, with the potential to produce more for export. She has a proven export record in such items as engineering products, textiles, whisky and computers. Granted self-determination, our fishing industry would be the most prosperous in Europe and we could become a major exporter of timber. We have the skills, the industrial capacity, the ports and the geographical location to become one of the powerhouses of the western world. At present, Scotland's oil is being drained away as fast as possible and Scots will be left with nothing to show for it. But under Scottish control, Scotland would be a major exporter of oil. By extracting it over a longer period, like Norway, we would spread the benefit and still ensure a yearly income of thousands of million pounds which would be used to redress the economic and social injustices that Scotland has suffered for too long. Invested in long-term development, these revenues would provide future generations with economic security long after the oil has been exhausted. Is such a policy one of greed and selfishness, as the Minister maintains? It is my belief, and I know that I speak for most members present in this Chamber, that such a policy is only to seek for justice. We need to make up for the bitter legacy of centuries of poverty, inequality, unemployment, emigration and cultural neglect."

Tam Linn paused and seemed to gaze at some point above the heads of his hearers, while mustering the words for his next statement.

"I believe," he went on in a voice charged with conviction and restrained emotion, "that, perhaps without fully realising it, we have today arrived at a crossroads in our national destiny. I think we are now faced with the need to make a choice between two ways. Either we must accept the Chamber's present emasculated status which Westminster is trying to impose upon us and hope that in the fullness of time a greater measure of freedom will be granted to us. Or we must decide that such acceptance is incompatible with the reality of Scotland as a nation whose potential and identity will only become realised with the attainment of full self-government. And this can only be through a truly Scottish Parliament entrusted with the sovereign rights of the people of Scotland. Six and a half centuries ago our ancestors were faced with such a choice — to accept domination by the English or to stand and fight for freedom. Today, a similar decision confronts us.

> *Now's the day and now's the hour*
> *See the front o' battle lour:*
> *See approach proud Edward's power —*
> *Chains and Slaverie!*

I say to Westminster — tak tent! Remember, the lion is rampant! Do not seek to frustrate the will of Scotland indefinitely, for time is running out. We have waited long enough!"

Rachel and I emerged blinking into the sunlight, to find a vast, ominously silent crowd packing the forecourt. All faces were uplifted, staring at the flag which snapped and fluttered above the Chamber Buildings. Gone was the Union Jack which had flown when Grimble arrived. In its place, blood-red on a yellow ground, streamed the Lion Rampant of Scotland.

"Maclean strikes again," whispered Rachel.

I nodded, thinking she was probably right. Suddenly I was oppressed by an unnamed sense of foreboding. The silent throng, the defiantly flapping Rampant, the distant, lowering bulk of the Castle all seemed to hint at dark, pent-up forces ready at any moment to burst forth with devastating consequences.

3
Flower of Scotland

A FEW DAYS LATER we found ourselves experiencing a further taste of that defiance whose growth seemed to accelerate with every new turn of events.

It took place at the annual Scotland versus England 'Big Match'. The occasion had always been a highly charged affair in the past and more recently there had developed an extra significance to the ritual clashes at Wembley or Glasgow. The date of the match this year was particularly unfortunate and there had been dire warnings voiced in the press about the consequences of letting the match go ahead. But generally it had been argued that contests on the field were a way of releasing emotions and preventing the battle happening in earnest. In the end this view won the day. Rachel had as usual been presented with a pair of tickets by one of her many good connections, so we drove over to Glasgow on a balmy May morning. I can't say that I was looking forward to the occasion. If I'd known how this match was going to turn out, I'd have gladly settled for a couple of rounds of golf at one of the many clubs where Rachel's connections seemed to rule the roost.

We arrived only minutes before the game was due to start. Rachel was unfamiliar with the new East End complex in which the ground was situated. The Calton Astrodome had been completed only some weeks before, and this was to be the first game to draw a capacity crowd. According to Rachel the game was being transmitted direct to a number of countries by satellite, a move encouraged by the local administration in Glasgow. Since this was now a safe Nationalist stronghold the venture was seen as likely to produce the confident, progressive image they cherished on television sets all over the globe. Even if Scotland lost the match there would be Olympic-style presentation of the vast auditorium in the astrodome, with its computer-controlled illuminated scoreboards situated in each corner of the building.

The whole astrodome project had been an exercise in political opportunism from the start. Intended as a placatory measure by Westminster to woo the Strathclyde voters away from the SNP, the project had taken far longer to complete than had been intended. By the time it was finished — a magnificent centrepiece to the redevelopment of the east side slums of Glasgow which a Labour Government had begun in the late seventies — the city was controlled by the Nationalists who therefore took all the credit. It had been openly stated in various sections of the press that because Westminster feared the same political reception for the Aukness Bridge they had vetoed funds for the project. It was maybe better that Grimble had decided not to be present as guest of honour today, as had originally been planned.

We took our seats on one of the long sides of the great oval as the two teams were emerging from the tunnel just below us. The roar from a hundred thousand throats was something I shall never forget. Amplified by the cavernous, blue-tinted plexiglass roof the sound had a harsh, primeval quality, the exultant snarl of some primordial beast newly risen out of its swamp.

Although the match was an all-ticket one and the ground had no terraces, within minutes scuffles had broken out between rival groups of young English and Scottish supporters. These were quickly separated by the newly-formed Sports Patrol who were equipped with heavy batons and moved quickly into trouble spots by means of purpose-built covered gangways that radiated down through the tiers of seats.

The action in the first half was frenzied and, despite my initial reserve, I found myself caught us in the excitement of the game. By the half-time whistle England were 2—1 up, vociferously supported by our part of the ground which seemed to be mainly occupied by those who had crossed the Border. During half time I looked up at a dizzying tidal wave of faces behind us, supporting a garish flotsam of scarves and Union Jacks.

From the opening of the second half England attacked incessantly, and all around us voices were baying with delight as the Scottish goalie became a punch bag for the England forwards. Some of the saves were unbelievable and to my mind that man was the hero of the match. This is not perhaps the high compliment it sounds, since elsewhere on the ground heroism was in short supply and the true spirit of sportsmanship seemed to be wearing perilously thin.

Then an England forward was brought down by a disgraceful body tackle only thirty yards from the Scottish goal mouth. To a deafening barrage of catcalls and roars of anger a free kick was given; it seemed that England would have a two-goal lead that must by then be unassailable, as the game was well into its last quarter. The goalkeeper must have had a sixth sense. Although the trajectory of the ball made it destined for the top corner of the net, it was stopped and held firmly. Hesitating only a second, the goalie made a long throw out to an unmarked winger. With the ball at his feet, he raced into the sparsely defended England half.

From then on the game took a completely different turn: the English attack had run out of steam and soon a magnificent header had drawn Scotland level. A roar broke out as the electronic scoreboards portrayed a Saltire flapping realistically above the score — a roar that was strangely muted on this occasion. It was all the more unnerving to feel that the temper of the mob was now harnessed and intent, waiting for the moment to unleash its full fury.

I have never felt at ease in a crowd of any size and this one seemed to be developing a new mood of sadistic exultation as the rejuvenated Scottish side played a game of computer-like efficiency. It was as if they were programmed to score the winning goal at a predicted moment. But I had lost all interest in the game; the ominous muttering of the crowd made my scalp creep and a hard knot grow in the pit of my stomach. I was beginning to wish that we had stayed away and watched the game on television like any civilised human being. The issue transcended the mere winning or losing of a game; it was now in deadly earnest. The despairing Cockney voices from up above us were clearly heard, as were raucous challenges from other parts of the ground. I glanced back over my shoulder and suddenly our position seemed as vulnerable as lambs in the shadow of a hovering kestrel. My palms were sweating.

Beside me, Rachel felt it too. "Nick, I can smell trouble," she said in her clipped, businesslike way. "As soon as the final whistle goes, let's make for the exit fast."

"Okay," I replied, trying to damp down the melodrama in the situation. "I don't think there's much cause for alarm, though. The police seem to have things tied up pretty tight." Even as I finished speaking I noticed four bright yellow vehicles like dustcarts moving to each corner of the field. On top of each one was a revolving turret from which a man controlled a water cannon.

Then the silence could no longer bear the strain. The jubilation that greeted the previous goal was drawing-room applause compared to this superhuman atomised sound. It was something totally new in my experience. African crowds can be noisily demonstrative and, if provoked or inflamed, unmistakably dangerous; but always, somehow, essentially innocent. There was nothing innocent about this eruption, and suddenly I discovered in myself the first symptoms of a mounting terror that could have become uncontrollable. Feeling asphyxiated and numb, I signalled to Rachel that we should leave now and began pushing blindly along our row.

I was stopped in my tracks by a concerted shout which burst from the tiers way above us. I looked up and saw a solid section of the crowd scrambling onto the benches. Hats and stocking-caps were whipped off, disclosing heads shaven bald except for a central crest of hair running from forehead to nape. On the other side of the astrodome, in the far distance, another block of supporters was also pulling off headgear, allowing shoulder-length hair — secured by scarlet headbands — to tumble free. Looking more closely, I saw that many carried crude coshes and missiles and — a more sophisticated addition to gang weaponry — "Morning Stars", consisting of wooden balls driven through with nails and secured to a short length of light chain. Pictures of the damage caused by this medieval throwback had recently been appearing in the more sensational sections of the press.

"Quick, under the benches," Rachel snapped.

Somehow that voice had the authentic ring of command and, almost without realising it, I had scrambled down beside her under the trestle seating.

"The London Apaches and Glasgow Mohocks out for each others' blood," she shouted in my ear. "And anyone else's for that matter," she added as our side of the ground was subject to a rain of missiles thrown over the barrier fence. "They're movements rather than gangs — something on the lines of the old Hell's Angels, but much nastier and twice as brutal."

Any further words were drowned by a thunderous drumming which grew to deafening intensity as the Apaches charged down over the stepped benches. As soon as this had ceased I raised my head cautiously and saw that the tiers above were littered with groaning casualties, some quite clearly needing urgent medical attention. As the full horror started to sink in, Rachel jabbed me in the ribs.

"Time for us to make excuses and leave, Nick."

Down below us on either side of the pitch the rival factions were piling up against the ten-foot crowd-resistant steel barriers separating the spectators from the ground. The water cannons had now opened up with solid jets of bright yellow dye directed along the line of the barriers and into the heaving mass now scaling them with ant-like singlemindedness. Suddenly portions of the steel mesh gave way with a harsh tearing sound and within seconds the pitch was flooded on either side by two yelling armies. The water cannons were lumbering into the narrow area of ground that separated the two sides, but I was sickened to notice that they were soon overwhelmed by sheer numbers. Each vehicle was rapidly surrounded by a screaming yellow wave and within seconds the driver had been pulled from the cab. A shaven-headed savage appeared in the turret and began to play the cannon on the Apaches below us.

As we struggled through the milling crowd towards the exit I felt shaken; I don't mind admitting it. In Africa I had several times been in tight corners against dangerous men or dangerous animals, but I had never encountered anything like this mindless, undirected urban violence. Rachel seemed to take it all in her stride, turning up her collar against the lurid spray reaching us from the turmoil below.

"Swinging Scotland," she remarked with a cool cynicism that amazed me, as she weaved her car expertly through the dense traffic leaving the area. In the distance we could hear the approaching sirens. "Grimble should have been there," she added. "He'd have got some idea of just how high feelings are running in the cities."

"I thought Westminster had climbed down a bit after the shindig in the Chamber."

"Oh, they made a few minor economic and fiscal concessions —purely cosmetic. The whole business of the Ultimate Prerogative and the basic control of the Scottish economy is as entrenched as ever. The Freedom Party and the Nats aren't fooled for a moment; Tam Linn's clamouring for blood again."

"The Fiery Cross people certainly seem to be active these days," I remarked. "You can't go down Princes Street without tangling with a Cran Tara rally or demonstration. I'd have thought that people would be getting a bit choked off with them."

"Don't you believe it! Cran Tara's just getting into its stride. Haven't you seen the opinion polls? They indicate a massive swing to the Freedom Party. Their influence behind the scenes seems to be spreading too. Have you noticed how many TV and radio programmes have been taking on a pronounced bias recently? Remember that programme where Cran Tara was compared with the brownshirts? Well, the director's out of a job now — don't tell me that's just coincidence."

Rachel's words were borne out by events as the elections approached. There was a widespread rumour that if the Freedom Party won a majority in the May ballot Tam Linn would declare some sort of UDI, a policy with which the SNP was quick to disassociate itself.

During all this time, as the clear, fresh spring drew towards summer, Rachel and I continued seeing a good deal of each other. Being fellow exiles provided a sort of bond and to some extent a common viewpoint. I made occasional visits to the Land Use Development Board, where Pringle had taken up the cudgels on my behalf, and became involved in a long correspondence over my application for UK citizenship. But mostly my time was my own and, as Rachel's working hours were flexible, we got into the habit of meeting for coffee, often followed by a stroll in Princes Street Gardens.

Our usual meeting place was the Horn, an amazing tour de force of fibreglass sculpture erected in Princes Street as the city's major cultural contribution to the Edinburgh Festival. It represented a gigantic cornucopia pouring out musical notes, supported by a straining Amazon, all studded with coloured lights. Although unmercifully criticised by professional aesthetes and the avant-garde set, it had quickly become a talking point for those passing by and now was generally referred to as Big Aggie.

Perhaps it was because up until now that I had spent my life in a predominantly male world, in which women had played an infrequent and decidedly minor part, that I was not sure how to take Rachel. I liked her frank personality and sardonic sense of humour. And through her I had gained a greater insight into politics, though I still viewed the whole set-up with scant respect. But at times I became intensely irritated by her — the continual need to analyse and assess different points of view, the joy she derived from unravelling the needless complexities in every situation — whether in politics or more personal areas. The position was made worse because I felt at a loose end, drifting from day to day. Unable to take to the dull city life, hemmed in by buildings and traffic, I was unable to get the opportunity to escape to a world where I could be once more in my element.

One Sunday we went tramping in the Pentlands, something I had been trying to persuade her to do for weeks. Although the day started off fine, a dense sea-fog came rolling in from the Forth and we got well and truly lost, blundering about for many hours in the thick haar before we struck a road. The Pentlands are a surprisingly wild range, considering their closeness to the capital, and I was surprised at how little I needed to encourage Rachel in most uncomfortable conditions. She bore up cheerfully and, when we eventually found the car, she showed less relief than I certainly felt. She assured me that she would come again, given the opportunity.

But by now the elections were on us and Rachel had to work all hours to provide coverage of candidates and issues She was syndicated to a news agency based in Lagos that relayed her articles to the press of what used to be called the "emerging black nations" in Africa. Since many of these had gained their independence within living memory, there was keen interest in whether Scotland would try to set a similar course.

4

Night of the Gaberlunzie Men

ON ELECTION NIGHT I dropped into a hotel bar at the end of Princes Street about the time the first results were coming in. It was a velvet-warm evening and the streets were busy with people leaving cinemas and theatres. Although it may have been pure imagination on my part, there seemed to be a charge of suppressed excitement in the air which communicated itself to me more strongly as an observer. Neither I nor Rachel was able to vote, but it was clear that polling stations had been deluged by a massive turn-out.

I had met Rachel for a drink at lunchtime. But it was not for long since she had to go over to Glasgow to prepare for the Election Special television programme later in the evening. I had not seen her for almost a week and had hoped to bring the talk onto more personal matters, but I saw from the outset that this was a lost cause.

"There are big things in the pipeline, Nick. I've been talking to the media people all morning and they're sure that it's the Freedom Party that's soaking up the votes. The SNP have just tried to be too flexible this time and have kept their options open too long. Look at that man Forbes, their spokesman on home rule; he can't utter a plain sentence on SNP policy without qualifying it in the next breath."

"But surely that's what most people want," I protested. "They don't want to take one big jump into the unknown; it's only natural to prefer a step-by-step solution. Surely it's only the extremists who are going over to the Freedom Party."

"No, you're out of date, Nick. The SNP lost the extremists years ago when they had eleven seats at Westminster and before they committed political suicide by bringing down the Labour government in 79. True, they've had a partial comeback since then, but they've never really recovered their old fire and drive. The Freedom Party have taken up their mantle. Now people are seeing that the only way to get change is through the Freedom Party, even if by unconstitutional means."

This really got under my skin. "But for heaven's sake, Rachel, we both know what happens when the pot really boils over. I'd still be in Kenya now if people had been able to think sensibly before they let in the Chinese."

"Oh, come now, Nick. You're conveniently forgetting a lot of past history; even if I agree with your analogy, surely you must realise yesterday's extremists are today's establishment?"

It was too hot to argue; besides it was clear that she was just sharpening up her wits on me in preparation for tonight's television encounter. She left shortly afterwards. I stayed on until closing time to soothe my armour-propre in the way of my new country.

I was still feeling fairly ill at ease when I plumped down in a comfortable armchair in the hotel foyer. A large television screen had been set up earlier in the evening and, with the added incentive of an all-night licence, it looked as if the hotel would do good business until well into the early hours. The place was soon stiff with politicos, many in full-dress kilts and sporting Cran Tara badges or SNP rosettes. Although the polls had closed hours ago they were still arguing the toss; I realised too late that I had come to the wrong place for a quiet night's viewing. However, by this time I was on to my third gin and tonic. Lacking the energy to move elsewhere, I gritted my teeth and stayed put, trying to concentrate on the screen which now flickered into life.

To my further annoyance the election programme was preceded by thinly-disguised Freedom Party propaganda. This one, to judge from Rachel's previous critisism, was probably more subtle than average but still below the belt as far as I was concerned. There were no words, just a series of visual sequences — workers in a steel plant, children playing street games, drilling operations aboard an oil rig, a hill farmer with his flock, a Highland crofter, a pipe band in Princes Street and a few snatches from some Highland games. As a herring boat sailed off into the sunset, evocative but vulgarised Scottish pipe music accompanied the caption "Scotland — our Country". This seemed to go down very well with all shades of political opinion surrounding me. I went to the bar to ask for some English beer.

When I came back the election programme had begun. The presenter was busy explaining in needless detail the method by which the state of the parties would be shown "to you, the viewers". Behind him a wall panel showed the names of the constituencies with columns for total votes cast for each party. Next to this there was a huge outline-map of Scotland, with the constituency boundaries marked in.

The proceedings opened with a series of statements from each party's representative on the programme. These seemed to become more verbose and self-congratulatory by the minute. Not having seen this type of programme before, I was amazed at the attempts of the presenter to sow the seeds of acrimony all around him, with the result that one or two tempers had shortened by the end of the first half hour. Rachel wasn't given much of a chance to intervene during this exchange of viewpoints; it was as if she and the lobby correspondent from a London daily were dangerous outsiders. Naturally I did not know anything about those on the programme, but the impression came across strongly that they knew each other only too well and they also knew how the public liked to see them.

Only at one point did I feel that Rachel might have cast aside these constraints. The SNP spokesman was being questioned by her about the difference in home rule policies between his party and the Freedom Party. They sparred for a few minutes and the man was countering very well against Rachel's sharp, clipped questions; he was certainly doing more promisingly than I had. Beginning to admire the man, I realised that it was he whom Rachel had dismissed so slightingly at our lunchtime meeting.

At last I could see that Rachel's anger was rising, something I had rarely seen before. It must have been a novel experience for her attacking line to be so unproductive; in cold print she would undoubtedly have carried the field, but the screen before us showed a confident, easy-going man of striking profile speaking with all the apparent wisdom of Solomon. Finally he won game, set and match. Rachel cut short one of his eloquent answers, blurting out: "But surely, Mr. Forbes, these so-called 'determinate aims' of the SNP will mean exactly the same as the Freedom Party's aim of total independence for Scotland. Both will ultimately result in some form of UDI."

There was an electrifying pause of ten seconds or so before Forbes made his answer. He looked straight into the camera and, speaking so softly that I did not realise he had lapsed into dialect, he said: "Och, lass, we want Independence everra bit as much as the Freedom chiels. But there's a sayin' where I come from — 'Words may when spurs will nae.'

You see, ye can sometimes get far more from a thrawn nag by persuasion than force."

There was almost audible back-slapping from the other political figures surrounding him. Rachel, realising that she could not compete in this sort of game, looked ostentatiously into a far corner of the studio.

"Ah, here we have the first results," the presenter chipped in, holding a hand to one ear. I thought I detected a note of relief in his voice.

The name of the constituency and those of the candidates, with the number of votes polled, were suddenly illuminated on the panel. The appropriate part of the map was now black like the missing part of a jigsaw. From then on the programme was a welter of figures and percentages, half-explanations and on-the-spot instant analysis. As the results rolled in, the empty spaces on the map were replaced by black, striped, squared and stippled areas. As predicted, it turned out to be a straight contest between the Freedom Party and Labour, with the rest out of the hunt pretty early on.

The atmosphere in the room became more charged. The early victories were toasted by each side, the Tam Linnites headed incongruously by a huge, kilted fellow who spoke with a pronounced Oxford accent. There were many cries of Sleanthe! accompanied by stamping of feet and spirited exchanges from one side of the room to the other. I was beginning to feel quite animated too.

By midnight the solid black and striped areas on the map looked almost equal and nearly every seat was now a close result. The Freedom Party's attack only seemed to have failed in the northern islands where Independent candidates won handsomely. By now it was two in the morning and a strong trend had established itself in the Freedom Party's favour, greatest support coming from constituencies in the Highland and Central Regions, the Western Isles, Strathclyde, Fife and Lothian. Results from Dumfries and Galloway, the Borders, Tayside and Grampian constituencies narrowed the gap occasionally, and there were a number of results which had been subject to repeated recounts and could have gone either way. But the map now contained large areas of sharp, diagonal black stripes.

Rachel had left the programme an hour or so ago and I was trying to think sensibly about whether I should phone her up. Feeling more than a trifle woolly-headed (and not relishing the prospect of being snapped at twice in the same day) I decided to celebrate with a double Scotch. All around victory toasts were already being proposed to an independent

Scotland and spirit glasses were hurled into the cavernous mouth of the empty fireplace. Others were muttering and slinking away out into the night. I decided that rapprochement was the best course and struck up a meandering conversation with one of the kilties who had also spent a few years in southern Africa. It must have been almost three o'clock when a page boy came round saying there was a call for me.

I weaved my way to the phone booth and shut the sliding door behind me, causing an infernal clatter.

"It's Rachel, Nick. I didn't think you'd still be there."

"Oh, I say Rachel, you really were something tonight..."

"Keep it for later, Nick. I think there's something funny going on. As I came back into Edinburgh about half an hour ago I noticed a lot of activity on the streets."

"Well, I expect Tam Linn's mob are pretty pleased with themselves. Perhaps they've already removed Sir Walter Scott and given his place on the monument to our Tam."

"For heaven's sake be serious, Nick. In the city centre there's practically no one on the streets. But there are troops everywhere. Buildings have been cordoned off and there are lights blazing in some public offices. On the North Bridge I had to stop at a road block while convoys of lorries and guns went up the Royal Mile to the castle."

I pondered this information owlishly for a few seconds then gave my considered reply: "Hold your horses, old girl. The army's been doing night manoeuvres a number of times these last few months; you've commented on it yourself. Now, it's been a hard night for everybody. Why don't we just get some sleep and see how the world looks tomorrow?"

There was an impatient snort through the earpiece. "Nick, I'll give you the credit of being drunk. You can't be that stupid."

As I struggled for a rejoinder she put the receiver down. I did likewise, pondering her words more seriously. Something stirred inside me, and suddenly some fresher air seemed like a splendid idea. I headed for the revolving doors leading onto the street.

The silence was surprising. There was no sign of movement the whole length of Princes Street. Opposite me the solid bulk of the Castle Rock loomed menacingly out of the night sky. From up there voices and heavy engines could be heard, sure enough, and shadows of men and machines thrown by the floodlights. But I couldn't convince myself that this amounted to much. Then there was the sound of heavy boots and voices coming up one of the paths from the depths of the gardens below the castle. Instinctively I retreated into the shadow of the hotel porch as a troop of figures in battle dress came up level with the street.

Soon they were moving purposefully near the foot of the Horn, which was a riot of coloured lights, giving off an air of carnival gaiety in the deserted street. They were near to Big Aggie's legs when I saw that one of the men, his hands protected by rubber gloves, was reaching up with a pair of wire-cutters. There was a blue flash and the Horn went dark.

As they moved on along the gardens repeating the procedure with every coloured flood, I felt my head spinning and gasped for air. There was a matter-of-factness about the way the Horn had been put out, almost a casual nonchalance. It struck like a mailed fist to the stomach.

5
Hodden Grey

DURING THE REMAINDER of that night and throughout the following day, as soon transpired, all the key institutions of public life underwent a series of brief internal convulsions. They had been infiltrated over a long period by leading members of the Fiery Cross. In published accounts celebrating this remarkable instance of Scottish guile those involved became known as the Gaberlunzie Men. A reporter with good connections amongst the Cran Tara had recalled that King James V had mingled with his subjects disguised as a wandering beggar or gaberlunzie, and the name stuck. The take-over of authority in the armed forces, police, central administration and the media was swift and total.

Within a fortnight the Tam Linn regime, by continually emphasising that it had a popular mandate for its policies, was in control of the cities. Although it had real power in its hands and, as far as could be seen, the oil revenues were also under its control, the regime stopped short at creating a provisional government and declaring independence. However, Westminster immediately took an uncompromising stand. At the time it was said that there was strong pressure from America and the EEC Council of Ministers for firm measures. This was due to nervousness over the fate of special trading agreements on oil that had been set up by Westminster some years previously.

Whether or not this was so, after a month of frenzied diplomatic activity between London and Edinburgh, an ultimatum came from Westminster. Unless the rebel 'government' surrendered its unconstitutional powers and economic claims by the fourteenth day of August forcible measures would be used to bring Scotland back within the framework of the United Kingdom.

It is at such moments of crisis that a great natural leader is apt to emerge — a Cromwell, a Napoleon or a Churchill. In a simple yet stirring speech, broadcast throughout Scotland and widely reported in the world's press, Tam Linn told the people their country faced the most crucial turning point in her history. There could be no compromise. Scotland must resist. Surrender would mean not only the end of hopes for economic prosperity but the end of Scotland as shaped by history. Westminster and Europe could never afford a recrudescence of the national spirit. This would have to be stamped out with a thoroughness beside which the measures of Edward I and Butcher Cumberland would appear as the work of amateurs. He concluded with a reminder and an exhortation, both of which had become household phrases throughout the country — "We gar'd them rin at Bannockburn. Stand Firm!"

This speech resulted in a wave of militant patriotism sweeping all parts of the country. Scotland had found a leader of the Bruce or Wallace stamp. Within days a Scottish Parliament (into which the Chamber swiftly transformed itself) had voted through special powers and a provisional government was rapidly constituted. Shortly afterwards recruiting centres were set up, to be swamped by volunteers. Within days Scotland had become a nation under arms.

But when the fuss and fury had died down life carried on very much as it had before UDI. Looking at the faces of shoppers or strolling lovers in Princes Street gardens I found it hard to believe that the tremendous constitutional upheaval of the past few weeks had actually taken place. There were rumours of plans to cut the main road and rail routes south at the Border and continual references in the press to troops training on Dartmoor, but it began to seem that the outside world was going to let the new state of affairs continue. In pubs and at cocktail parties one heard over and over again confident evocations of "the English sense of fair play" or "Westminster turning a blind eye". Others referred in lower tones to the phoney war.

The first shock to the confidence of the new 'government' came when the London papers announced that Shetland was taking measures to secede from representation in the new Scottish Parliament and to petition for direct Westminster rule. The loss of the oilfields in Shetland waters would have dealt a savage blow to the credibility of the Tam Linn regime. Although the reports were never officially confirmed, a delegation was sent to "get round a table" with the Shetlanders. Amongst all the other events in a rapidly developing situation of crisis this piece of news was quickly forgotten.

For now the new government was starting to implement the reforms and changes of policy promised in the Freedom Party manifesto — control of Scottish affairs to rest with the Parliament, withdrawal from the EEC, dissolution of regional government, and radical reforms of social legislation and taxation. As expected, Westminster's veto on the Aukness Bridge was now annulled and every day commitments were made to press on with this and other large-scale industrial projects.

As people in Scotland began to realise and accept the new situation the mood of uncertainty and foreboding was replaced by a buoyant, outwardlooking spirit of optimism. Posters and leaflets began to appear. Typical was one showing factory and farmworkers, housewives and office girls, students and old folks all arranged in a pyramid formation, smiling broadly. At the apex was an idealising portrait of Tam Linn, looking youthful and at the same time impressively sagacious. The caption to this one read 'Our Folk — Our Future'.

Other posters showed him on a farm holding a lamb, or with his arm around a little girl with red hair, or shaking hands in a muscular fashion with helmeted workers on an oil rig. Despite the traces of ballyhoo and sentiment in this propaganda, I think it did echo in quite a telling way the aspirations of many at the time.

Of course, Tam Linn's every word and action was utilised by the media and his qualities were eulogised on every possible occasion. There was no doubt that he genuinely inspired widespread respect, even starry-eyed love. Catchphrases like "Oor Tam" or "Tam's the Lad" crept into everyday speech. Though not succumbing to this universal euphoria, I was broadly sympathetic to the new order. I had known a number of countries where independence had only been achieved by considerable bloodshed; this more peaceful path I was prepared to follow until events warned me that things were turning nasty.

About this time I received a letter asking me to call again at the Land Use Development Board offices. This time Pringle had good news for me regarding the cattle ranch project. On a wall map he indicated an area inland from the Moray Firth, south-west of Tomintoul.

"Carnafarry. Gie the place a look over then let me ken what ye think. If you see possibilities then I'll recommend personally that ye get the backing ye need. If ye dinna make a go o'it then you're no Ned Wainwright's son."

Vastly relieved to be exchanging the political hothouse atmosphere of the capital for the clean winds and open space of the Highlands, I set about arranging my journey. Rachel offered to give me a lift north: it would give her an excuse to take a break at her retreat near Braemar. As this wasn't so far from my destination, she could drive me to a point near to the gamekeeper's cottage on the Carnafarry estates where I was to stay.

Rachel had been saying lately that she was feeling washed up and sick of the insidious propaganda that had to be cut through in order to file relatively truthful stories. A few days' rest in rural surroundings would help to recharge her batteries; and it seemed like a great opportunity for both of us.

On a brilliant August morning we drove north over the Forth Road Bridge. I felt as eager as a schoolboy on holiday, but Rachel seemed flat and preoccupied. It became apparent a very few miles north of Edinburgh just how much military activity there was; military vehicles were passed on the road north every few minutes. At one point a great pipeline came snaking down a hillside to dive under the road by a culvert. "The pipeline from the Tay-Tummel-Rannoch reservoir complex," Rachel said drily. "It took water to the north-east of England until Tam Linn turned off the tap."

After Blairgowrie the scenery changed dramatically, flat farmland giving way to mountains and rolling moor covered in heather just turning purple. From Deeside with its noble stands of trees we could see away to the north-west, rising above the lesser peaks, a great massif which I guessed was the Cairngorms. My first sight of the Highlands brought back stories that my father had told me when I was being put to bed as a child in Kenya.

A few miles beyond Deeside we turned a bend to find the valley ahead crawling with troops engaged in manoeuvres. Many wore the new pinkish grey uniform of the Scottish Republican Army. This Hodden Grey was the colour of field dress in pre-Union days.

We were flagged down by two very young soldiers who demanded to see our identification cards. They made a great show of checking the documents, then made us get out of the car while they proceeded to search it, making more or less open references to the fact that we were strangers from south of the Border, as they thought. Then one of them started frisking Rachel. The sight of his hands working over her slim body suddenly made me see red.

"Cut it out," I snapped.

The youngster turned to face me. His callow, freckled face tried to assume an expression of sneering toughness.

"An' whit'll youse dae aboot it?" he retorted.

"Listen, sonny," I grated, keeping my voice as level as possible. "If you weren't so wet behind the ears I'd wrap that rifle round your neck. You wouldn't be able to stop me — your safety catch is on for a start. Call yourself a soldier! And stand up straight when I'm talking to you."

A soldier instinctively responds to authority. I hadn't lost my old army touch and inside a minute both lads were standing up straighter, with burning cheeks and shifty eyes, while I gave them a savage dressing-down for sloppiness, lack of discipline, and general unsoldierly conduct. I swear it was all they could do not to salute as we drove on our way.

The incident left me feeling a bit concerned on Rachel's behalf. I didn't like the thought of her tangling with that sort of situation on her own.

"Look, Rachel," I said. "I'm not too happy at the idea of you staying alone in the cottage with all these troops on the prowl. I think you'd better come and stay with me while I'm at Carnafarry. You can have the bed, if there is one; I don't mind dossing down on the floor."

Rachel drove for another half-mile before making an answer. I was beginning to wonder if I'd overstepped the mark.

"Got it all worked out, haven't you?" she replied at length, her voice holding an edge of suppressed fury. "Mister high and mighty Wainwright lays down the law. Such smug bloody arrogance; there are times when you're insufferable, Nick. You enjoyed cutting down those two kids back there, didn't you? Well, just don't try shoving me around, that's all."

I listened to this stream of diatribe in absolute amazement.

"Hey — you've got it all wrong," I began, then looking at her face I realised it was hopeless. She had a look of utter defiance that would allow no argument. But the next minute she might produce a flood of tears if she were really upset — you never could tell with Rachel. I broke off with a shrug.

We continued the journey in a prickling silence. The final lap to Tomintoul was along one of General Wade's roads, built to allow redcoats to patrol the turbulent Highlands in the eighteenth century. The gridiron pattern of the little town, with its stores and hotels, gave it a Dodge City appearance; I was later to remember how peaceful it looked on that evening.

We crossed a broad river, the Avon, and drove past a large house where there were groups of soldiers standing around. We then took a minor road that went along the side of a spectacular canyon, reminding me of the dried-up riverbeds or *wadis* that you get up on the Kenya-Somalia border. Finally, in the late afternoon, Rachel dropped me off where the road petered out, within a mile or so of the boundary of Carnafarry. I collected my things and got out of the car.

We said goodbye awkwardly. The sound of curlews all around us and the feeling of peace, as a glorious summer's day subsided into evening, were spoilt by the gulf that now separated us. The seconds lengthened while I looked at her finely-moulded African profile and tried to find appropriate words. But they wouldn't come, and finally with a sigh she started the car and drove off without a wave or backward glance.

6

Enemy HQ

I DON'T think I have ever been so utterly content as I was during that next week. I believe there is a Robinson Crusoe inside each of us fighting to get out. Tramping round my kingdom, measuring, observing, taking notes, seeing in my mind's eye herds of cattle stippling the hillsides — all this seemed to fulfil some deep, primitive urge, perhaps an instinct handed down through generations of Wainwrights. The gamekeeper's cottage was spartan enough — oil lamps and bare stone — but I didn't mind that, being used to much more primitive accommodation on occasions in Kenya. I had brought hiking clothes and equipment and enough tinned food to last a week.

On the twelfth of August — a truly Glorious Twelfth, for once — I was out on recce as usual. About midday I flung myself down on the hillside overlooking the canyon of the River Ailnack, that I had noticed on the day of my arrival. I extracted lunch — a can of beer and a tin of bully beef — from my sidepack and was about to pull open the tab on the beer can when I noticed a man walking on the road above the canyon. He was too far off to make out details clearly, but he seemed to be wearing city clothes which struck me as odd garb for the terrain. He was also walking warily. I fished out my binoculars from my pack and focussed them on the figure. Yes — natty blue pinstripe. And something about the man seemed familiar. The ruined, once-handsome face, the lean, elegant figure — where had I seen them before? I tried matching the man's appearance with people I'd known, then with film stars, actors, TV personalities, politicians, army pals. Suddenly it clicked — Harris! The man's face had been in all the papers several years previously, in connection with a big espionage affair. Playboy Harris, a well-known London society figure and holder of a key position in the Ministry of Defence, had been selling military secrets to the Russians for many months when MI6 got onto him. Harris had just managed to make a getaway to Russia in time. In Moscow he was milked of information (it was presumed) then sent out on missions as a travelling stooge to further anti-western propaganda.

Studying his face through the glasses, I saw it suddenly tighten and a look of fear enter his eyes. A large motorcar coming from the direction of Tomintoul appeared on the road below. It bucketed along till it came up with Harris, then two bulky men scrambled out and closed in on him. I was too far away to hear their conversation but, judging from the animated gestures of the two big fellows, it didn't seem a particularly harmonious one. A few seconds later all three got into the car which then swung round and drove furiously back the way it had come.

What on earth was Harris doing in this romote part of Scotland? The little scene I had just witnessed suggested that he was under some kind of duress, or at any rate, restraint. I had been on too many safaris in the African bush not to feel a stirring of the hunter's instinct. There could be no harm in a bit of stalking on my part. This wasn't just idle curiosity. In my book, anyone who sold his country's secrets was just about the lowest form of life around, and I felt vaguely that in some way I would be shirking by duty if I turned my back on the incident I had witnessed. I was pretty sure that I hadn't been noticed. I followed the contour round the shoulder of the hill keeping the road in view. The car drove into the grounds of a large house near the confluence of the Ailnack and the Avon, the house that I'd noticed when driving up with Rachel. I wriggled myself down in the heather so as to be invisible from the house and trained my glasses on it. It was a massive structure, built in what I believe is called the Scottish Baronial style. Soldiers appeared in the grounds from time to time and sentries, regular as clockwork, kept circling the building.

The afternoon dragged on, hot and interminable, but waiting was a trick I'd long ago learned to master, on safari in the Northern Frontier District of Kenya. The world swam in an amber light and the air was heavy with the scent of heather. Apart from the occasional call of a curlew there was utter silence. I managed to keep sleep at bay by devising little tasks, like counting the number of pepper-pot turrets and windows I could see. At last, after a mulberry gloaming, such darkness as comes to northern Scotland in high summer drew in and I moved down the hillside to a better point on the edge of a wood beside the road.

From my hiding-place I had a clear view of the house. On the side facing me was a courtyard with three huge cages whence sounded the rattling of chains. In addition to guard dogs there were the sentries: two figures passed each other in the courtyard every fifteen minutes, before disappearing through archways in the containing walls. They carried what looked like automatic rifles.

I had no definite plan beyond the intention of somehow getting into the house and eavesdropping. I began to get cold feet and speculated about what sort of mess I would be in if I were to get caught. But there was no future in thinking along those lines and I forced myself to concentrate on the immediate business. High up on the wall above the courtyard a stone balcony projected in front of what looked like a french window. That might have possibilities. There was no direct way of getting onto the balcony but a fire-escape on the same wall gave access to the roof. Once on the roof it shouldn't be difficult to work along it to a point above the balcony, using the gutter as a foot-rest. After that it wasn't much of a drop to the balcony.

Time to go. Now that the moment for action had arrived, a tingling excitement filled me. My senses seemed curiously heightened so that I was sharply aware of the smells and sounds of the night — scent of pine and heather from the cooling earth, the distant purling of the river, a night-bird's cry. I scrambled over a brick wall, ran through a vegetable garden at a crouch and reached the bottom of the fire-escape.

I was halfway up it when I heard feet crunch on the gravel drive below me around the corner of the house. The guard was ahead of schedule! I froze — any movement, even the tiniest scrape of my commando boots on the iron rungs might give me away. For a few seconds I was sure he had seen me, then I heard a match sputter and smelt cigarette smoke. I prayed that the guard would move on, but presently he was joined by his pal. The two of them nattered on interminably while I stood barely three yards above their heads, trying to persuade myself I could somehow vanish if they looked up.

Glancing down, I saw that the one with the cigarette was a big, burly fellow. His companion was smaller, but stockily built.

"Tomintoul's a sight better than Balmoral," the big one was saying. "Plenty of booze and burds here, eh?"

"What like is it at Balmoral, then?"

The hefty guard spat disgustedly. "Bloody monastery. Come to glorious Deeside," he parodied in the manner of a holiday brochure, "Live in a storybook castle set amidst the rugged grandeur of the

Hielans. Thrill to the squawk of the grouse and the hum of the midge."

"Heard the clash aboot an invasion — Westminster sending an Expeditionary. Force?"

"Aye," replied the other truculently. "Smash the Mahdi stuff. Teach the Fuzzies a lesson, chaps. The bastards are just waiting for the amnesty to run out — the day after tomorrow."

The two guards separated and continued their rounds. Painfully, I resumed my climb and soon lay panting on the roof slates. When my muscles were sufficiently relaxed, I began to crawl crabwise along the roof, using the gutter to support my feet. I eased myself off the roof until I was hanging from the gutter by my fingers, then dropped four feet to the balcony and fell back against the parapet with a thump that winded me.

Facing the balcony was a french window and the room inside was dark. I tried the handle, but it was locked. I was considering my next move when lights went on in the room beyond. I shrank back against the wall in the narrow space between the edge of the window and the parapet. Then I heard the sound of the window being unlocked.

I felt sure someone must have heard me land on the balcony and was coming to investigate. But the seconds passed and nothing happened, so presumably the window had been opened to air the room which would be stuffy after such a hot day.

I peeped cautiously round the edge of the casement, and found myself looking into a large drawing-room which had been hastily adapted to become a military headquarters. Filing cabinets stood against the map-hung walls and on desks stood telephones, typewriters and piles of paper. Drawing up seats round a table in the middle of the room were none other than Tam Linn, Harris and a big, cheerful-looking, snub-nosed man dressed in the new greyish-pink Hodden Grey uniform of the Scottish Republican Army. I recognised him at once — 'Daft Davie' Campbell, Commander-in-Chief of the Republican Forces. Colonel, now General, David Campbell had earned the soubriquet Daft in pre-UDI days for the panache and originality of his command in action. I had read somewhere how he had dispersed a rioting mob in Ulster by stampeding a herd of shorthorns at them, then charging home with the local fire engine, both hoses firing.

Tam Linn was speaking and I could hear his words plainly — words that were soon to induce in me a horrified disbelief.

"That was a stupid thing to do," he was telling Harris. "Wandering off up the glen like that. Your face is well-known — suppose someone had recognised you?"

"There wasn't a soul besides myself out on the moors," was the sulky answer. "I only wanted to get away on my own for a bit. You can't know how precious privacy becomes if you haven't lived behind the Iron Curtain. There was no need to have me fetched back." Harris' voice broke. "Oh God! How I hate living like this — guarded every second of the day, unable to move in any direction without some watchdog trailing me." He began to sob. "It's hell, I tell you — pure hell!"

"Ach! get a grip, man," said Campbell, not unkindly. He splashed whisky from a decanter into a glass and pushed it towards Harris, who gulped it down in one swallow. "What's past canna be mended. And ye're bein' weel paid. That's some consolation, surely?" He looked across at Tam Linn, his eyebrows raised questioningly. "Weel Tam, we maun send this chiel back tae his maisters wi' an answer o' some kind. The Deal's on, I take it?"

Tam Linn looked straight at me, a frown creasing his fine forehead and his mouth set resolutely. I knew of course that the light in the room made me quite invisible, yet having his gaze upon me was a disquieting experience. I have felt the same sensation before when watching some animal I have been hunting: on at least two occasions I could have sworn the animal bolted because it sensed my presence though it could neither see, hear nor scent me. I prayed that Tam Linn didn't possess any such hyper-awareness.

"Aye, Davie — the Deal's on," he said heavily switching from Standard English to dialect Scots. "The sair truth is we're a wee nation and we canna stand on oor ain indefinitely agin England, gin she's backed up by the Community and likely NATO. We havena the smeddum tae resist economic sanctions or large-scale military invasion. The Celtic Union boys in Wales and Ireland are keen tae help but there's no muckle they could dae ayont sendin' a wheen guerrilla contingents. You that's a military man will ken better nor me that wi'oot aid we couldna haud oot verra lang."

"Aye. We havena but the yin choice," agreed Campbell. "Either accept the Russians' offer o' trading agreements and military aid in return for permission tae build rocket and missile-firing submarine bases. Or go under. Mind, I'm no feared aboot this Expeditionary Force they're sendin'. Yon's chicken feed — nae mair nor a recce in force, ye might say. We ken pretty weel where they're gaun tae land and their strength — thanks tae your idea o' infiltrating a Gaberlunzie intae the War Office in London. We ken the strike'll be somewhere on the Moray coast, within a thirty-five mile radius from here. Wi' all the forces we've concentrated, I've nae doot we'll gie them a bloody neb. Ach! if it was only the English on their ain we had tae worry aboot, we could tell the Russians tae get lost."

"I'm wondering," said Tam Linn, "if, wi' an English presence off the Nor'-East coast o' Scotland, the Shetlanders 'll no mebbe try something."

"Nae fear o' that. If Maclean says the Shetlands are pacified, then pacified is what they'll be — and what they'll stay. When yon man does a job, he doesna do it by halves. Mind, some o' the lads I sent wi' him were jist a wee bit squeamish at the things they had tae dae. Ach! but ye canna mak an omelette wi'oot breakin' eggs, as the English say."

I experienced a thrill of horror. 'Pacified' I suspected was a euphemism for something pretty drastic, if Maclean had any hand in it. Now I knew why secession had been such a shortlived issue.

Further details were discussed — the Russo-Scottish Agreement would be privy to a small cabal of Gaberlunzies in the Council (the ruling party's Cabinet) and a few high-ranking officers in the armed forces. Harris would return for the answer on the eleventh of September in a calendar month less one day, to allow time for unforeseen possibilities to materialise, such as England deciding after all to recognise the Scottish coup. In which case Scotland would no longer have any need of a pact with Russia. A copy of the proposed Agreement, giving full details, was taken from a box file on the table and given to Harris. A buzzer was pressed and the two bruisers who had hunted him down on the moor arrived to escort him away.

Tam Linn and Campbell moved over to one of the wall maps and began to discuss plans to counter the Expeditionary Force. After about fifteen minutes they too left.

I would never get another chance like this one. With a pounding heart I slipped through the french window, crossed the room and opened the box file. Inside were documents similar in appearance to the one handed to Harris. They were printed in some sort of code and I had no doubt that they were all copies of the Agreement. I removed the top copy — it was about the size of a government White Paper — and stuffed it into my side-pack. Then I returned to the balcony.

It was beyond my athletic powers to climb back onto the roof. From the balcony to a flower bed below was a long drop but I landed without mishap. Unfortunately I must have dislodged a piece of cement or loose stonework from the balcony's parapet, for something bounced off the grass beside the flower bed and rattled on the stone flags of the courtyard.

Almost immediately a clatter of chains exploded from the dog cages, then silence. The dogs themselves made no sound. Either they were muzzled, or — and my skin crawled at the thought — they were Doberman Pinschers! Pinschers — the mute black killers used by the Gestapo in manhunts and the Kenya Police against Mau Mau. They would rip out your throat in a flash. Without bothering to take cover I streaked across the yard, scrambled over the wall and began to pelt up the road above the Ailnack canyon.

I slowed to a walk after a few minutes, feeling fairly certain that I hadn't been noticed or pursued. But a minute or two later a swift padding from behind made me turn my head. An enormous, shadowy form was bounding towards me. I experienced a moment of paralysing fright. Then, as happens when you've a charging buffalo in your sights and are trying to hold your aim, the brain clears and my nerves steadied.

Summer nights in the north of Scotland are not really dark and soon I could see the animal clearly enough — a Doberman Pinscher as I'd feared. It was the size of a calf, carrying a muzzle crammed with vicious fangs. My mind raced. A scene in a feature film about police dogs being trained flashed through my brain — a man trying to shake off an Alsatian whose jaws were clamped to an arm protected by padding. I looked round for a branch or stone to serve as a weapon. Something gleamed at the side of the road — a lemonade bottle. I smashed it on a stone to produce a nasty weapon. Swiftly I dumped the contents of my sidepack on the road, wrapped the sidepack round my left arm then tied my sweater round on top.

Next moment the brute was on me. With a frantic resolution I thrust my left arm out in front of my throat as it leapt. I felt its teeth pierce through the improvised armguard and a stab of pain shot up my arm. I staggered under the impact. Then, recovering, stabbed at its neck with the shard in my fist. A mad fury washed over me. Again and again, I drove my weapon into the thing...

The mist cleared from my brain. The Pinscher, its head and neck horribly mangled, lay twitching on the road. Jets of blood spurted blackly from its throat. Trembling with reaction, I disengaged the bloody padding from my arm, dragged the carcass to the edge of the Ailnack canyon and shoved it over. My arm was bleeding from a row of black holes and I had started to dab at the wound with my handkerchief and when I heard the distant noise of shouts and running feet coming from the direction of the house. Hastily I refilled my mangled sidepack, tied the bloody sweater round my waist and took to the hillside.

As I headed homewards at my best pace, my mind raced in top gear, taking stock of the monstrous information I had come by, and devising a plan of action. If the deal with Russia went through, Scotland would become a Cuba-in-Europe with unthinkable implications for the balance of power between the Western and Soviet power blocs. Detente, that most precarious of institutions, would be blown to smithereens. At a time when NATO's southern flank was crumbling, her northern system of strategic communications would be threatened with disruption. Scotland, because of her oil and her geographical position, was the vital link in the chain. And that link would be snapped if the Russo-Scottish Agreement were to become fact.

My own part was clear. I must warn Westminster well before the dead-line, September 11th, so that they could act in time to prevent the deal from taking place. If the Expeditionary Force failed (and neither Tam Linn nor Campbell seemed particulary worried about it), a fullscale military invasion would probably not be launched for several months, at least. And in the meantime...

It was providential that I had been able to steal a copy of the Agreement, otherwise who in Westminster would believe me? It would take more than an unconfirmed story by an immigrant ex-colonial to persuade the Westminster and NATO authorities to act immediately against Scotland.

There were several possible complications I would have to take into account. First, my departure from the house had been noticed. It was quite likely that I had not actually been seen, and even if I had been, there was no reason to suppose that I was anything other than a prowling tramp or hiker. But it could only be a matter of time before the Dobermann was found. My theft of the document might not be noticed for some time, but equally it might be discovered at any moment — in which case a tight security net would be drawn over the whole area. So I was going to have to get out fast. Unfortunately there were two hundred miles of hard country between me and the Border. At a stretch I could manage it on foot, but I'd be a fool not to try other, faster ways of transport first.

I decided that I'd try to catch a southbound bus, if there was one, from Tomintoul. Failing that, I'd phone Rachel from a call-box in Tomintoul and try to get her to give me a lift to Edinburgh. She could be my only way out of this situation, although I didn't want to get her involved unless I had to.

Strangely, my predominant feeling was not one of consternation or alarm, but of disillusionment. By one impetuous act my own dreams of a Highland cattle ranch were now in ruins and my vision of the splendid young Leader, who was to bring his country to a glorious future, had proved to be one of an idol with feet of clay. Only now did I realise how strong his influence had been on my outlook.

Having made sure I was not being followed, once back at my base I closed the shutters before lighting the oil lamp. I examined my arm. Blood was still welling from the punctures but the wound didn't look too serious. I washed, disinfected and dressed it.

I felt vaguely that something was missing from my person. Glancing down, I realised with a pang of loss what it was — the small ivory amulet that I wore round my neck was gone from its thong, presumably torn off during the fight with the Pinscher. It had been the gift of an old African who had safaried with me in southern Tanzania. It was carved to represent a head and was to the old man the personification of his guardian ancestors. So bestowing it on another must have been a very real sacrifice. I would miss it greatly.

Suddenly I felt horribly alone and vulnerable, as though in losing the amulet I had myself been deprived of some protective influence. Angrily, I suppressed such imaginings: the thought crossed my mind that perhaps we Kenya-born whites are more African than we know.

My torn and bloodstained sweater and sidepack I discarded and buried in a peat hole near the cottage. I pulled on a fresh sweater. The time was now past midnight. I decided I had better take everything I might need for travelling on foot in case any snags over transport developed.

Apart from food I was quite well equipped for my trek. I pulled on an anorak and my strongest jeans — soft, close-fitting and faded as jeans should be — then replaced my hiking boots. Socks, handkerchiefs, underclothes and spare jerseys I crammed into the bottom of my rucsac. Then mending gear, dubbin, torch, whistle, an old pain of *velskoen* (in case my boots gave out), toilet gear, matches, mess-tins with spoon, dishcloth and tin-opener inside, a battered old pewter beer mug bearing a VR stamp — which a Nandi headman had given me for saving a sick cow — sleeping-bag, some polythene sheeting to improvise a bivouac and, at the top, my cape. Provisions didn't take up much room. I was almost out of them and had planned to get more from Tomintoul in the morning. Into the side-pockets of my rucsac went two tins of corned beef, a tin of sardines, a packet of Macvita, a few ounces of oatmeal in a polythene bag and a blessed half-packet of Lapsang Soochong tea —Lapsang that aristocrat of beverages, which can transform even the simplest of meals into an occasion. Silva compass, forty pounds in paper money and the vital Agreement I stuffed into my anorak map pocket. I inserted an old touring map of Scotland and my OS map of the Cairngorms into the map case.

Then I buckled round my waist a belt to which was attached, in its sheath, my old Bowie that had been my best friend in the bush. I'd shaved with it, chopped firewood, used it to hack a path through hellish wait-a-bit thorn, and once killed with it when jumped by a bunch of murderous nomads at a water-hole up on the Ethiopian border.

I eased on my rucsac. Then I blew out the light, locked the door and set out for Tomintoul.

It was still dark when I reached the little town. I had no idea when the next southbound bus was due to leave, but some early-rising local would no doubt be able to enlighten me. I settled down to wait in the porchway of a store in the wide main street. I must have dropped off to sleep for an hour or more, for when I suddenly found myself nodding awake buildings were emerging greyly in the first light.

7

The Drums

IT WAS LIKE a scene from a Western — the wide, empty main street with hotels and stores slowly materialising in the dawn. To complete the picture all it needed was the appearance at either end of the street of two figures, hands hovering above revolver-butts. And then something winked in the shadows on the far side of the street.

My eyes, trained through long experience to pick out the form of a stationary animal camouflaged against grass or foliage, focussed on the source of the tiny flash. Where a second before there had appeared to be nothing, a soldier materialised between two buildings. He held a grounded rifle with fixed bayonet, whose blade must have reflected momentarily a ray of early sunlight.

My eyes quartered the street and I eventually counted eight soldiers, all well concealed and as still as statues. No need to ask myself what they were there for, I thought grimly. There was still plenty of darkness about and, with my experience of stalking game, getting clear of the place undetected wasn't a problem.

The trick is to move only when you're sure of not being seen, and to keep totally still otherwise — it's movement that gives you away every time. Slipping from shadow to shadow, when none of the soldiers was looking my way and keeping absolutely motionless in the intervals, I worked my way out of the danger zone. In the same way I had once penetrated a herd of buffalo and brought down the old bull I was after, before any of the beasts knew what was happening.

Once clear of the main street, I made for the open country. My discovery of the soldiers at Tomintoul put a new complexion on things. If Campbell's men were watching the roads in the locality, it would be folly to try to get Rachel to collect me in her car. Besides, I didn't want to land her in possible trouble. I decided that my best plan now was to head south across country until I was well clear of the area within which a hue and cry might be expected, then to find some means of transport to the Border. I thought it unlikely that Campbell could be on to anything yet. The presence of those soldiers at Tomintoul probably meant that he just wasn't taking any chances. I studied my maps: I would trek to Deeside and the A93, from where it might be safe enough to take a bus or hitch-hike to Perth. Or, if I could contact Rachel once I got to Deeside, she might pick me up from there. Once in Perth, I would head for Edinburgh and the Border. I reckoned the riskiest part would be getting to Deeside. If I could get that far, I thought my chances of winning out were probably quite good.

Picking up the Ailnack, I followed it upstream or south, ploughing through heather and an occasional patch of prickly juniper. Now and again a grouse exploded at my feet and whirred off with its demented call of 'go-back, go-back, go-back'. I climbed up the crest of a ridge to my right, which I then followed. Barring one or two valleys which cut across the ridge, the ground rose steadily. At the same time the terrain improved till I was striding along on a marvellously firm surface of gravel, carpeted by short, springy heather.

It was a glorious sunny morning, with a bracing tang in the air thanks to the altitude. A vast, empty landscape of heather-clad moors rolled around me, silent save for the distant baa-ing of sheep or the whistle of golden plover. Away to my left the Ailnack Canyon cut a dramatic gash across the terrain. The whole scene bore an astonishing likeness to parts of Kenya I'd known — the Kinangop or the high Masai country.

By mid-morning I found myself on the summit of a high, bald hill set in the angle where the east-flowing Caiplich swings sharply north to become the Ailnack.

It was going to be a long day and I would have to stay as fresh as I could manage. I reckoned I could risk a short sleep. My position was a bit exposed but it had the advantage of commanding a superb view of the surrounding country. I pillowed my head on my rucsac then, setting my mental alarm clock to wake me in a couple of hours, I fell asleep.

I woke to find myself staring into the face of a curious sheep, which tore off the moment I stirred. The sun was well up in a cloudless sky. I felt stiff but not cold, although I was two and a half thousand feet up. All around me rolled a fantastic vista of moorland and distant blue summits, some with strange shapes like dromedary humps or whalebacks. Somewhere a dotterel called. A line of red deer switchbacked along a ridge and vanished.

I scrambled down to the Caiplich bank past a Gothic complex of rock pinnacles, aptly named The Castle on the map. Then, a wash and shave, using my Bowie as razor and a mess-tin for mirror. Next a spartan breakfast of scandy (oatmeal mixed with cold water) and two dry Macvita biscuits.

I saw from the map that if I headed due south I would reach Glen Avon in a few miles. I could then follow a path westwards along the glen to the intersection of another path which would take me south through Glen Derry and Glen Lui to Deeside and the A93 to Perth. It all looked extraordinarily simple on that idyllic summer morning. I felt free and able to take up any challenge I was offered.

My spirits began to rise and I found myself almost beginning to enjoy the adventure. My provisions should see me through — just. Barring lack of tent, I was well enough found. My funds were more than adequate to secure food and transport. Of course it was always possible that I might make contact with invading Westminster forces before then. Altogether, regarded as an initiative test, my task seemed something which a self-respecting Cub Scout could have taken in his stride.

After cleaning my mess-tin with grass and gravel, I crossed the Caiplich dryshod by stepping on boulders. Once over, I felt that I had crossed some kind of Rubicon. I toiled up a steep heathery slope to emerge on a plateau all fissured by peat hags, with occasional low, rounded summits swelling above the surface like sandbanks at low tide. Throughout the forenoon I worked my way steadily southward on a compass bearing. It was a tedious business picking one's route through the peat hags. Wherever a detour wasn't possible you had to charge down into the thing, hoping your impetus would carry you to the far bank before you bogged down in the black, clogging mess. On the summits, where water could drain off, the going was superb — hard-packed gravel cushioned by heather and cloudberry.

At midday, hot, tired and thirsty, I stopped for a break beside a stream. It was bliss to have the pack off. Munching Macvita, I foraged over a large area for dry heather to make a fire. Of all fires the heather fire must surely be the most tiresome. Heather burns furiously but is consumed in seconds, so you need to gather a small haystack of the stuff before striking the first match. I was lucky enough to find some fragments of Old Caledonian Forest poking like bony fingers through the peat blanket. This burned quite well and much less rapidly than the heather and in only half an hour I was able to brew up a mess-tin of delicious Lapsang Soochong.

It was shortly after I had resumed my trek that I became aware of a faint rhythmic sound in the distance ahead of me. The sound gradually grew louder until I realised what it was — drumbeats. Not long after first noticing the noise, I reached the lip of Glen Avon, a great gully with a fair-sized river brawling over a rock-strewn bed far below me. Several hundred feet below where I stood, a path ribboned along the side of the escarpment.

I slipped off my rucsac and wriggled forward to the edge of the slope, where I commanded an almost bird's eye view of the path. The rattle of the drums sounded quite close now and seemed to be coming from the west.

Suddenly to my right the head of a column of men marching in single file along the narrow track appeared round a shoulder of the hillside. They carried packs and guns — mostly rifles, though some had light machine guns. Like the soldiers at Tomintoul, they wore pinkish-grey uniforms, theirs appearing several shades lighter through being powdered with dust.

All through that hot afternoon, the long line of young soldiers, grim and formidable in Hodden Grey, filed eastwards below me. Between every hundred men there was a break and each section had its own drummers who tapped out a fast marching step. From their silence, vigorous step and precision in keeping station, I judged morale and discipline to be high. I guessed that they were heading for Tomintoul to swell the anti-Expeditionary forces mustered there. The thought again occurred to me — should I stick around and try to make contact with Westminster forces? A mental picture of myself blundering about in a combat zone, perhaps getting captured by the wrong side, decided me to stick to my original plan.

I waited a full half hour after the last drumbeat had died away in the distance, then scrambled down to the path and stepped out, following the Avon upstream in the opposite direction. Keeping to the hill, I would have been safer from detection than on the path, but I didn't trust myself not to get lost among the tangle of desolate summits between Glen Avon and Deeside.

I had travelled about three miles when the path, marching with the Avon, made a great turn to the south. The gully walls fell away and the path led down to the Avon which here flowed through a broad valley. After passing a deserted bothy the path became swampy and indistinct though still traceable, thanks to cairns piled up by considerate hikers. The evening was beginning to draw in so I made camp on an islet in a bend of the river overlooked by stony bluffs — Spion Rocks on the map.

I took stock of my island — it was about twelve yards long by eight wide and separated from either bank by ten to fifteen yards of water, shallow enough in places to wade across quite easily. By now I was exceedingly hungry and could have eaten all my provisions there and then. Prudently I rationed myself to the tin of sardines, a precaution I was shortly to be grateful for. Reluctantly I abandoned an attempt to gather heather for a fire. The ground in the flat valley bottom was too soggy for there to be much dry stuff. Missing my Lapsang tea, I studied the sky with slight foreboding. The weather was still clear and warm with enough breeze to keep the midges at bay, but streaks of cirrus cloud were growing in the sky. I took a final precautionary glance round the scene — a boggy strath contained by ugly rock-strewn slopes — and crawled into my sleeping-bag.

Rain on my face woke me up. Two o'clock in the morning of the fourteenth of August. I fumbled in my rucsack for my two spare lengths of polythene sheeting — the third was already in use as a groundsheet. I spread polythene over myself, using the heavier items of my gear to hold them down. The result was an unhappy hybrid between a tent and a coverlet. To get complete cover from my transparent carapace, I had to retract my six feet, tortoise-fashion. The rain increased till it was hammering down in torrents. Miserably, I listened to its drumming while water trickled through gaps in my shelter.

With a twinge of alarm I realised that the noise of the river was much louder than it had been the previous evening. Did the island get submerged when the river was in spate? Would I be able to wade to the bank at daybreak? I grew increasingly wet, cramped and wretched as the hours crawled by. My anorak, proofed though it was, began to let in water under my cape. Fortunately I had stowed away my partially sodden sleeping-bag to prevent its becoming totally saturated.

At last the interminable night drew to an end. As soon as it was light enough to see what I was doing, I crawled out of my sopping lair to take stock. With dismay I saw that my island had dwindled during the night to perhaps two-thirds of its original size. Even as I paced its juddering perimeter, a great section slid into the river. There was no question of wading or even swimming back to the mainland. Between the island and the banks raced a boiling flood of brown water with tumbling boulders surfacing like porpoises.

The rain became heavier. By noon my island had shrunk noticeably further and I became seriously alarmed. If the rain continued for very much longer my terra firma would simply disappear beneath my feet.

As always, my morale lifted after shaving. Beneath my polythene canopy I studied the map, checking route and distances. I ate one tin of bully beef which left me with one further tin, some Macvita and a fair amount of China tea. I calculated that it wasn't more than a day's trek to Derry Lodge, a mountain rescue post at the mouth of Glen Derry, not very many miles from Braemar. These mental exercises helped to keep my anxiety about the island from developing into panic. When the rain began to let up a bit I felt that the worst was over and, as there was no question of the river going down for some time, I settled down for a sleep.

I woke to find water pouring onto me through a rift in my shelter. Far from abating, the rain had increased to a solid downpour. I poked my head out and saw to my horror that the island was almost awash. Spate or no spate, if the rain didn't stop soon I was goint to have to swim for it. I couldn't get any wetter so I packed my polythene sheets and huddled beside my rucsac to wait, like some traveller at a railway station in wonderland. Came the evening and no easing of the rain. The thought of the island going down beneath me in the night was far from pleasant.

The toll taken by the mental and physical strain of the past two days must have been greater than I knew. Sleep was the last thing I intended but I woke suddenly to find myself sitting in darkness with water sloshing over my boots. After my initial panic I could have shouted with relief for the rain had stopped. Worry slid away from me like some physical burden and I drifted off to sleep again.

When I next opened my eyes the sun was high in the sky. The island once more stood clear of the water. The river though still in spate was dropping fast. I reckoned I might get across in the afternoon. I unpacked and undressed and spread my sodden gear and clothing to dry in the sun. I was famished and recklessly wolfed my last tin of bully. My stock of provisions was now a few Macvita and the precious Lapsang. What the hell! Once off this accursed island I'd make Derry Lodge or even Deeside

in one long haul. I was glad to discover that the thick webbing of my map
case had kept my notebook dry. I jotted down the date — August 15th —
and dozed off.

I woke up, vaguely aware of something having disturbed me. I looked
round and immediately flattened myself. A column of grey-clad soldiers
was winding up the valley towards me from the south-west. To my
dismay they halted directly opposite my island and began to pitch camp
on the flat ground in the bend of the river. Everywhere tents popped up
like mushrooms. Sentries appeared on Spion Rocks less than half a mile
distant which commanded a bird's eye view of my island. I couldn't get
off the island without being noticed and if I stayed I was almost bound to
be spotted by the sentries sooner or later.

But the hours dragged past and I remained undiscovered, even when
two soldiers came down to the riverside within yards of where I lay.

"Reckon we'll miss the fun?" asked one, filling a canvas bucket from
the Avon.

"Aye. Ah doot we'll no be needit," replied the other, a stocky red-
haired chap. "I've heard tell that Oor Tam and Daft Davie kenned where
the Redcoats wis gaun tae land. They'll hae caught the bastards wi' their
breeks doon, maist like."

My only hope of avoiding detection was to keep absolutely still. I
managed this without too much discomfort till mid-afternoon, when a
dreadful thing happened. The breeze died away. Anyone who has been in
the Highlands on a still, humid day in August knows what this means —
midges! They materialised from the heather in countless thousands and
battened on my exposed body so thickly you could scarcely have put the
end of a finger between them. The tickling and biting grew unbearable.
Only by a huge effort of will could I restrain myself from slapping at the
crawling film that covered me.

I knew that any movement on my part would put me in deadly peril of
being spotted by watchful eyes on Spion Rocks. I thought of the hours of
daylight that still remained with despairing horror. I had experienced
some trying times in the fly-ridden bush of Kenya's Rift Valley, but
never anything to compare remotely with this torment. The midges
launched a concentrated attack on face, neck and extremities, biting
away with persistent viciousness for hour after hour. The discomfort was
appalling; to this day I don't know how I summoned the strength of will
to stop myself from brushing the pests away. There were times when I
began to wonder if I might not go mad under the strain of keeping still.

But at last, after an eternity of torture it seemed, it grew dark enough to draw on my clothes and slap at the midges in safety — an unimaginable relief.

As soon as it was fully night I put on my boots, eased on my rucsac and lowered myself into the river. The water swirled up to my waist as I waded towards the north bank and I nearly lost my footing several times on shifting boulders. At last I reached the bank and after hauling myself onto land, followed the river upstream keeping close to the bank to avoid blundering into the camp. When its scattered lights were far behind me, I struck off to my right, aiming to work along the ridge forming the north side of the glen. In this way I would avoid the risk of bumping into any outlying detachments.

After the enforced inactivity of the island, walking was a pleasure and the wind caused by the motion kept the midges away. After a stiff climb I reached the crest of the ridge and looked back to check my position in relation to the camp. But the lights had all vanished. I stood shivering in the cooling wind that had begun to blow up the glen, my brain in a whirl. Then a great bank of shimmering whiteness surged up out of the glen towards me.

8

The Haughs O' Cromdale

DAYBREAK DISCLOSED a spectacular sight. The ridge on which I now sat rose like a gigantic whale above the sea of mist that resembled cotton-wool. In every direction for as far as I could see rolled a white plain studded here and there by summit-islands. With map and compass I tried to orientate myself but eventually had to admit that I hadn't the faintest idea of where I was. The jumble of peaks didn't seem to fit anything I could recognise on the map.

Reasoning that if I headed south again I ought to intersect the Avon, I set off on a compass bearing in that direction. My course took me down into the mist. Stumbling blind through the whiteness was an eerie business. After several painful encounters with boulders I was forced to slow down to a crawling pace. The near-elation I had felt at the start of my journey was being eroded by discomfort, hunger and a most unpleasant sense of disorientation. I could begin to sympathise with travellers from England in the pre-Walter Scott era who found the Scottish Highlands 'horrid' and 'melancholy'. Long-forgotten fragments of Fraser Darling, read by a comfortable fireside during my first days in Edinburgh, floated up to the surface of my memory — blanket bog... extreme Alpine conditions of our Central Zone... arduous U-shaped glacial valleys... Lairig Ghru... Black Mount. These once innocent-sounding phrases now had a sinister ring to them.

Eventually I came to a tiny lochan whence issued a south-flowing stream. I followed this down a steep slope. Gradually I became aware of rushing water below me, and in a few minutes I stood on the bank of a biggish river which I might well have walked into in the mist had it not been in noisy spate. Surely this was the Avon. After walking upstream along the bank for about a mile I came across a little hut made of boulders, constructed by sea cadets according to a stone plaque above the lintel. I checked the map. Yes, there was the hut at the head of Glen Avon and there should also be a bridge. Now it existed only as a few broken piers poking above the swirling water.

I crawled gratefully into the boulder hut. Oddly, although I was exhausted I couldn't sleep, but simply to rest in shelter and to know where I was did wonders for my morale and physical condition. I shaved and entered the date, August 16th, in my notebook. Food was what I needed most, but there was hardly a scrap left.

Shortly after noon rifts began to open in the mist bank, revealing tantalising glimpses of scenery like fragments of an uncompleted jigsaw puzzle. More and more pieces fitted into place, then the last of the mist shredded away, revealing the finished picture — a rolling grassy plateau at the centre of a crossroads where four glens met. Wading carefully from pier to pier of the vanished bridge, I crossed the Avon not without difficulty. I realised my strength was going. Picking up the path on the south bank, I headed into the southernmost of the four glens, leaving the Avon at last behind me. Shortly after passing two gloomy lochans my numbed senses appreciated that the upward trend of the terrain was levelling out. With a quickening sense of excitement I realised that I was approaching the great watershed between Speyside and Deeside. With perfect timing the sun broke through, suddenly transmuting a sodden wilderness into a sparkling world of silver and soft green. Minutes later I crossed the height of land and looked down on Glen Derry. I was trembling with fatigue. I have a pretty tough constitution but hunger, exposure and prolonged foot slogging were beginning to take their toll.

On my right hand gaped a huge corrie — undoubtedly one of Fraser Darling's Arduous Glacial Valleys. This opened into a long wide glen, stippled with woods at the southern end — a welcome sight to my tree-starved vision. I plodded down the glen on a graded path with the Derry Burn on my right. My clothes dried quickly in the hot sun and a pleasant breeze kept my old friend the midge at bay. My spirits began to rise a bit. Near the mouth of the glen the path crossed the Derry Burn by a neat metal bridge — erected by engineering students from Aberdeen University, so an inscription told me — then wound through noble stands of Scots Pine. I was so engrossed by the magnificent trees with their strange twisted limbs and bottle-green foliage, that I failed to notice figures closing in on either side.

I was jerked brutally out of my reverie by the sudden apparition of a bayonet at the end of a rifle which materialised in front of me. It was held by a young, tough-looking soldier in the now familiar pinkish-grey battledress. With a sick, hollow feeling, I glanced round and saw more soldiers stepping from the trees all round. Feeling like a paleface who has blundered into a redskin ambush, I continued along the path with the soldiers keeping station beside me.

Not a word was spoken till we reached a complex of huts and bridges at the confluence of the Derry Burn and another large stream, the Lui Water. The mouth of the glen was a pleasant place of glades and gravel beaches. Everywhere were tents with soldiers moving among them. I received many curious stares and sensed an atmosphere of aggressive excitement about the whole encampment. The leader of my escort roughly ordered me into one of the huts. I complied with a shrug, feeling that to protest at this stage would be futile and possibly dangerous.

I sat down on a bench at the far end of the hut, watched by one of my captors assigned to guard me. I tried to put up a front of cool nonchalance but my heart was thumping and my palms beginning to sweat. I felt weaker than ever and inclined to give up the whole show. Above all I felt the Agreement burning a hole in my anorak map pocket. At any moment I might be searched and that would be that. It was my guard who gave me the opportunity I needed. He rolled a cigarette then felt in his pockets vainly for a match.

"Ye wouldna hae sic a thing as a licht, pal?" he asked.

I forced my mind to work feverishly. Before producing matches from my rucsac, I made a show of searching my anorak map pocket, managing to roll up the Agreement and shove it up my sleeve. Then while the guard was busy lighting up, I slid the thing into the wastepaper bin beside me. The problem of recovering it later would just have to be played by ear.

What a bloody fool I'd been to get myself into this mess! I should have reckoned that mountain rescue posts might be occupied by soldiers. I ought to have moved along the heights overlooking the glen instead of marching down the path. My only excuse was that exhaustion had eroded my alertness and powers of concentration. I decided that when they questioned me my best course would be to give a true account of my circumstances and movements as far as possible, without giving anything away. To try to build up some elaborate alibi would be hopeless. I would tell them about my journey north and my sojourn at Carnafarry. I would say that I had gone walking and got lost: I had been benighted in the hills and had been blundering about in the mist until it cleared, when I set off to look for some habitation where I could find rest and food and be able to work out my exact location. Wasn't it lucky for me that I had met up with them and could I be on my way please?

If they hadn't found the dead dog, if they hadn't discovered that an Agreement was missing, if they didn't examine the bite marks on my arm, if they didn't wonder why I had included a sleeping-bag but no tent in my baggage, then I might be off the hook. Too many ifs, I thought, lapsing into despair again. My eyes began to close...

I jerked awake as a sandy-haired little fellow with steel-rimmed spectacles and a gold thistle embroidered on his sleeve bustled into the hut and, sitting behind a folding table, fired questions at me. He industriously scribbled down my answers — most of it was the sort of stuff that appears on Income Tax forms — then he asked me what I was doing in Glen Derry.

I gave the edited account of my activities as planned.

The little man proceeded to cluck and preen himself like a self-important hen. "Aweel, ah dinna ken," he muttered, shaking his head and pursing his lips. "It a' soonds a bit unsatisfactory like. Ah think ye'll hae to dae better nor that. We've been asked tae keep a look oot for onybody suspeecious."

"Look, you can easily check up on me," I said, beginning to feel desperate. Clearly, this pocket Robespierre was enjoying the vicarious importance derived from detaining me, too much to let me go before milking the situation of its last drop of dramatic benefit. "You can contact the Land Use Development people in Edinburgh. Ask to speak to a Mr Pringle. He'll vouch for me." I felt my resistance weakening and wished for sleep more than anything.

"Hut, man. It's no just that simple," he said sententiously, in the tones of a bank manager turning down a request for a four-figure loan. He jabbed a forefinger at me. "Furrst, ye see, there'll hae to be an offeecial enquiry. Ye're frae Africky, sizyoo, strollin' intae Fort Derry the day efter oor lads has beat the Expeditionary Force at Cromdale. Ah, but jist supposin' ye're an escaped Redcoat or an English spy? Ye soond jist like an Englishman tae me. Yin o' thae toffee-nosed buggers frae —"

Outside, a swelling roar of welcome was building up into a rhythmic chant — "Oor Tam! Oor Tam! Oor Tam!"

"I'd best report tae Tam wi' this in person," muttered Sandy importantly, and bustled out with his papers.

I began to nod and, despite the hardness of my bench, must have dropped off to sleep within seconds of Sandy leaving the hut. I may have slept for two or three hours before being wakened by a soldier saying that Tam Linn wanted to see me.

I was escorted to a small stone house standing apart from the huts and shown into a room filled with Hodden Grey-clad soldiers. In their midst towered a red-bearded giant in a Fair Isle sweater. The room fell silent and all heads turned to look at me. I desperately tried to appear unconcerned.

This was the first time that I had seen Tam Linn close up. The strong mouth, shrewd eyes, the mane of hair above the cliff-like forehead — all seemed somehow larger than life. The man emanated energy in an almost tangible way. I felt I was in the presence of a natural force, like a waterfall or a volcano. Our eyes met and I felt the impact of his personality almost as a physical shock.

"Well, well — the roving rancher," declared Tam Linn in a bantering sort of way. Once again, I was struck by the guttural, curiously resonant quality of his voice. "Welcome to Fort Derry. I've been reading a report about you."

For several seconds he fixed me with his keen, penetrating gaze. I felt uncomfortably that he was seeing right inside me and laying bare my innermost secrets. I felt a strange overwhelming compulsion to tell this man everything, to release into his keeping the great burden of hardship and responsibility imposed by my secret mission, that was crushing me with its weight. But with a great effort, I forced myself to return his gaze steadily and to remain silent. Strangely I found myself unable to define the colour of his eyes. Were they green? brown? blue? hazel? It was impossible to say.

"Perhaps your story's true, Wainwright," Tam Linn said at last, musingly. "Perhaps not. Anyway, you'll stay here till I've made up my mind about you. Meanwhile Sergeant Docherty here, my Household Bodyguard, will be responsible for your safe keeping." And he nodded towards an immensely squat barrel of a man with a grotesquely large head, who semed vaguely familiar. He put me in mind of a mad Lorenzo de' Medici. His oversized features, built-in grin and air of latent aggressiveness combined to form a distinctly unpleasant impression. I put his age at about twenty-three or four. Suddenly I remembered where I'd seen him — with Maclean beside the rostrum in the Meadows, where I'd first heard Tam Linn speak.

"Let's go, English." Docherty's voice held a horrible gloating familiarity. He escorted me to the back of the house and locked me in a storeroom. Shelves filled with blankets, uniforms, entrenching tools, mugs, mess-kits etc, lined the walls. I was provided with an iron bed, a table and folding chair and my rucsac was returned to me. Docherty then proceeded to frisk me expertly. Fortunately, he didn't tamper with my bandaged arm.

"I gather there's been some fighting since the amnesty ran out on the fourteenth," I observed, thinking that any information I could glean from my captors might prove useful.

"There has that," Docherty said with relish. "The English landit on the Moray coast. Supposed tae be a secret operation but it seems their security wisna verra guid. They cam' doon the road frae Lossiemouth in a motorised column. Oor lads wis waitin' for them at Cromdale." Docherty's eyes gleamed and he smashed a fist into his palm. "Man, whit a hammerin' we geid them. It was Johnny Cope a' ower again. They pu'd oot and awa' back tae their boats. Aye, Westminster'll no forgit the Battle o' Cromdale in a hurry." He broke into a falsetto giggle which, issuing from that gross body, sounded obscene. It was the sort of noise a sadistic infant might make when pulling the legs off flies.

Before leaving, Docherty picked up an enamelled iron mug from a shelf. He cradled it in one hand and began to squeeze. Chips of enamel flew from the stressed metal. There was a crackling sound and the mug suddenly crumpled in Docherty's fist.

"Jist in case ye get ony ideas, English," he chuckled companionably. He dropped the crushed container on the floor and left, locking the door behind him.

I sat down on the bed and tried to plan. Things didn't seem to be going too badly and it looked as if I might be released in the fairly near future — provided the time-bomb ticking away back at Tomintoul didn't go off first! Somehow, I must contrive some stratagem to get the Agreement back from the wastepaper bin in the hut.

At nine o'clock Docherty unlocked the door and conducted me to a stretch of level ground beside the river. "We're celebratin' Cromdale. Tam Linn says ye're tae be allowed tae jine in. Dinna try onythin', chum," he leered, "or Ah'll pu' the lugs affa ye." Again that dreadful falsetto giggle.

I shuddered. I had the feeling Docherty might be as good as his word. I have always been able to give a good account of myself in a fight but taking on Docherty would be like tangling with a gorilla. There was something about the fellow that gave me the creeps — not just his brute bulk and strength, but a quality of gloating malevolence that set a familiar chord vibrating in my subconcious.

Everywhere were soldiers of the Scottish Republican Army. Some were roasting meat over barbecue pits. Crates of beer were being distributed. Fortunately a breeze to keep the midges away was blowing. I was treated to curious stares and mutterings. "It's yon bluidy Sassenach," I heard someone remark.

Strolling from group to group, chatting, swopping jokes was Tam Linn, the banter and laughter always loudest in whatever circle he joined. Spotting me, he waved me over and we settled down with a dozen others on log seats round a barbecue pit. In the friendliest way he drew me into the circle so that any suspicion and hostility towards me melted away. Steak, sausages and beer were pressed on me. I was intrigued by Tam Linn's bilingualism — in the most natural way he talked broad Scots with the soldiers, whereas with myself he used Standard English.

Presently, two young soldiers appeared in the midst of the assembly carrying guitars, and proceeded to tune up amid shouts and banter.

"Those lads iss The Two Geordies," the soldier next to me remarked, in the lilt of the West Highlands. "Grand singers. They wass on the telly chust afore UDI." The resemblance to Maclean's inflection made me shudder unwittingly, and I remembered the expression in Docherty's features.

And grand singers they were. They performed with terrific drive and gaiety, their voices harmonising in the most pleasing way. Their repertoire was folk songs, mainly Scottish. We had 'The Hills o Gallowa', 'Tatties an Herrin', 'Coulter's Candy', 'The Bonnie Ship the Diamond' and 'The Wark o the Weavers'. Then they launched into The Gomerils' great hit — 'We gar'd them rin at Bannockburn'. The audience went wild and, led by Tam Linn, roared out the chorus —

> *We brak the English on yon plain,*
> *And dang them doon wi' micht an' main,*
> *And we sal dae the same again,*
> *As on yon field o' glory!*

I reckon myself to be a pretty phlegmatic type on the whole, but that night I found myself irretrievably caught up in the mood of wild exhilaration and sang with as much gusto as any. I experienced a flash of understanding of the mad battle-fury latent in the Scottish character —

the ferocity that appalled Hanoverian troops in the Jacobite campaigns
and earned Highland regiments the nickname Ladies from Hell in the
Kaiser's war.

The climax of the evening was a rendering by The Two Geordies of
'The Haughs o' Cromdale' — a stirring ballad commemorating a
seventeenth-century battle between clan forces and government troops.
Nothing of course could have been more appropriate and the audience
howled for encores.

At this juncture a soldier cam hurrying up to Tam Linn to say that
there was an urgent radio message for him. Half-way through the second
encore a summons came for myself and Docherty to return to the stone
building.

When, a few seconds later, I faced Tam Linn there was an expression
in his eyes I did not care for. He extended a closed fist towards me, then
opened his fingers. On his palm lay a familiar small round object, a
carved likeness of an African's head — the amulet I'd lost during the
fight with the Pinscher.

"I see you recognize it, Wainwright," he said in tones which sent
what the Scots, I believe, call a 'cauld grue' through me. "Just been
brought in from Tomintoul. I rather thought we might establish an
'African Connection'. The radio report mentioned other things that have
just come to notice. There are subject of mutual interest we must discuss
— dead dogs and missing documents for a start. I'll look forward to
hearing a full explanation in the morning."

9

Hide and Seek

I MADE a thorough inspection of the inside of the storeroom, but there was absolutely no way out. The single window had been heavily shuttered from the outside and the door was a massive solid affair quite beyond my powers to break down. Docherty had removed my Bowie knife, so I couldn't tinker with the lock or door hinges. I switched off my torch to conserve the batteries and tried to think.

It was only too clear what had happened. The amulet — an obvious lead to my identity — had been discovered: in the ensuing brouhaha not only had the dead Pinscher been found but the theft of the Agreement had come to light. So all was up unless I could contrive to escape from Fort Derry before being interrogated. I couldn't break out of my prison, so my only hope seemed to lie in being able to overpower Docherty. As he was supposed to be keeping me under observation, I could expect a visit any moment. I had to admit that my chances of getting the better of Docherty on a purely physical basis were probably about as high as those of a Pekinese defeating a Great Dane. Still, like everyone he must have an Achilles heel. My only chance lay in being able to discover and exploit it.

A minute or two later the key turned in the lock and Docherty appeared in the doorway, an electric lantern in his hand. "Weel, English, ye're for it noo," he gloated. He entered my prison and locking the door behind him leaned companionably against the wall. "Ah'll be there tae help if yere memory need joggin'." He gave his appalling giggle.

I switched on a shaky grin. Trying to sound cowed and apprehensive — it wasn't too difficult — I murmured, "I expect you're quite good at helping people to — ah, remember things."

"Aye. Ye could say that," Docherty confirmed with the modest pride of a good workman in his skill. He flexed his sausage-like fingers, looking at them as a craftsman might regard a favourite tool.

"You know, Docherty, I find you interesting," I went on. "When I first set eyes on you, I could see that here was a man of action — the type who *does* things rather than merely talks about them. Am I right?" Steady on Wainwright, I warned myself. You're laying it on a bit too thick even for this ape.

"Weel — Ah'll no say different," conceded Docherty. Then an extraordinary thing happened — his eyes half-closed and a redness slowly suffused his grotesque face. I realised with a start that he was flushing with pleasure at my compliment!

"Yes — I'm seldom wrong in summing up a man," I added sagaciously. I now decided to take a calculated risk. If it misfired I was done for. If it came off Docherty might be hooked. "I can admire someone who takes a direct line," I continued, "even if he's on the other side, so to speak. Perhaps I shouldn't say it, but this leader of yours — Tam whatsisname? well, he seems a bit too intellectual for the sort of game he's supposed to be playing." I gave Docherty a knowing look. "If you see what I mean."

"Do Ah no!" growled Docherty with feeling. A thunderous scowl wiped the flush from his features. "Him and yon walkin' skeleton Maclean. Aye yatterin' aboot books an' ideas. Whiles it makes ye want tae voamit."

My ranging shot had hit the target! I had guessed what Tam Linn, perhaps because of the very bigness of his outlook had probably never suspected. Docherty, whom Tam Linn most likely regarded as a faithful bulldog, was eaten up with jealousy and a sense of inferiority. I imagined Docherty's background — tyrant of the school playground, asserting himself over teacher's pets who eclipsed him in lessons by beating them up: later as king among the corner boys, gaining status by grabbing old ladies' handbags and assaulting solitary pedestrians. The ego of such a dunghill cock, accustomed to being first in the pecking order, would be flayed raw by daily exposure to a personality like Tam Linn's, especially when a rapport existed between Tam Linn and the intellectual Maclean.

"I bet you could show them a thing or two when it came to unarmed combat," I suggested innocently.

"Ye've said it, pal," replied Docherty. There was a dreamy look on his face as though he were acting out some mental fantasy in which Maclean was doubled up screaming as a result of a karate chop from Demon Docherty.

"I used to know some little tricks myself," I murmured diffidently. "I expect you'd be surprised if I told you I was champion three times running in the Nanyuki elbow-wrestling contest."

"Is tha' a fact?" said Docherty appraisingly.

"Scout's Honour." I ran my eyes over Docherty's tank-like build as though assessing strength and fitness. Jutting out my jaw, I laid down the challenge. "I'm not sure I couldn't take you."

"Ach, dinna talk sae daft!" retorted Docherty. 'Ah could push yer airm back wi' twa fingers."

"That's easy enough to *say* of course." I made him feel he'd been slow to take me up.

Docherty reddened. "Come on an' Ah'll show ye!" he snarled, putting his lantern on the floor. "Pit yer airm on the table."

We sat facing each other, myself on the bed, Docherty on the folding chair, our right arms locked forearm to forearm on the table. Docherty looked like an enormous, evil toad, exuding self confidence and malevolence. I felt the hairs on the back of my neck prickle. I have known real fear only occasionally in my life and now was one of those times.

"Right English?"

As my arm arced helplessly towards the table, I sprang the surprise I had been planning. My right foot lashed out under the table to connect with the folding chair. Simultaneously, my left hand whipped a spiked entrenching tool from the shelf beside me and crashed the side of it into Docherty's temple.

The folding chair collapsed and Docherty sprawled on the stone floor. He sat up groaning and holding his head. In a frenzy of desperation I hurled myself on top of him and grabbing his hair, started banging his head on the flagstones. I just couldn't bring myself to use again the entrenching tool, all blade and spike.

Presently reason returned to me. Docherty was no longer groaning. Bleeding from a gash in the head, he had gone limp and his breathing was heavy and laboured. I bound and gagged him with strips torn from a blanket, removed the key from his pocket, scooped up my rucsac and let myself out. I turned the key in the lock and pocketed it.

I tiptoed past the main room, which showed a light under the door and crept out of the building. For once I blessed the midges. The breeze had died and the pests were out in force, consequently no one was about. I crept to the hut where I had hidden the Agreement and found the door locked. I broke a window with a stone, sweating as the glass tinkled on the floor inside, pushed my hand through the hole and released the window catch. After climbing through, I rummaged in the waste bin and to my enormous relief found the document still there. I stuffed it into my rucsac where it would be more protected from the elements than in my anorak map pocket.

Minutes later I was clear of Fort Derry, hurrying back up the path towards the head of the glen. Ignoring the subtleties of double bluff, I reckoned that my best chance of avoiding recapture was to head in the opposite direction to that which I would be expected to take. If I swung west up the great corrie I had seen that morning, it should lead me into the heart of the Cairngorm Mountains. In their remote fastnesses I might be able to throw off pursuit, then eventually detour round and head south for the Border again.

As I pounded up Glen Derry, I reflected on my situation. It was pretty desperate. Tam Linn simply couldn't afford to let me get away. When my escape was discovered, in an hour or two at most, a relentless manhunt would be launched. Oddly, the realisation of that fact steadied me. I am, I think, a reasonably peace-loving citizen. As long as people leave me alone, I'll return the compliment. But I don't take kindly to being shoved around. Right, Tam Linn and the rest of you, I said to myself, you'll have a run for your money. The challenge was, in a strange way, exhilarating and I found myself relishing the situation.

Two hours later the mouth of the corrie gaped to my left and I struck off into it up a fork of the path. The gradient steepened and soon my breath was coming in laboured gasps. My back and leg muscles began to protest against the pack weight and the punishing slope. My earlier near euphoria evaporated. Sweat poured from my face and back and soaked my anorak below the armpits. After about a mile I came to a concrete Memorial Hut and staggered inside to rest and check my bearings on the map. Screening my torch with a handkerchief so that no light would issue from the window, I studied the map and saw that my present route would lead me to a spine of land connecting Cairn Gorm and Ben Macdui. To the west of Ben Macdui the terrain fell away into a long deep pass called the Lairig Ghru. The farther side of this great gully was a winding ridge whose highest points formed the peaks of Braeriach and Cairntoul. Westwards again stretched a tangle of glens and corries, contained by Strath Spey to the north and Glen Feshie to the west. These 'Badlands' seemed well suited to my purpose. So Westward Ho! then. My only plan at this stage was to shake off my pursuers. Eventually I would try to head for the Lowlands through the wild and lonely country to the south of the Cairngorm massif.

Then a most disquieting thought struck me. My total stock of provisions consisted of a few Macvita biscuits and some China tea. It would be hard to imagine an area more utterly devoid of food than the one I was about to enter. I told myself that the ill-effects of lack of food were largely psychological, that I could easily subsist for several days on my biscuits. But this was cold comfort. Eventually, I would have to raid outlying settlements to replenish my supplies. At least I had a full stomach at present, thanks to the barbecue at Fort Derry.

I continued to slog up the corrie. It was much colder than in Glen Derry, presumably because of the increased altitude, and the midges had accordingly disappeared. The slope steepened alarmingly and the going became gruelling in the extreme. My pack, despite its lack of provisions, felt as though it were filled with stones. My breath became a sort of tortured panting and sweat glued my underclothes to my skin. Yet whenever I stopped for a breather, the sodden patches chilled instantly and within seconds I was shivering with cold. After what seemed an eternity, I struggled over the lip of the corrie and stood with trembling legs on level ground.

A grimly magnificent scene stretched before me, washed by the light of the moon, which had till then been masked by the wall of the corrie. An amphitheatre of crags ringed a glittering sheet of water — Loch Etchachan. Beds of eternal snow flecked the rock faces. Now and then icy draughts slammed down from the heights to ruffle the surface of the loch. Above the cliffs to my left the dark mass of Ben Macdui loomed like some mis-shapen monster. Everywhere enormous boulders littered the slopes. It seemed I had penetrated into some Arctic and inhuman world.

A wave of exhaustion swept over me. In my sleep-starved state I knew that, unless I could find somewhere soon to bed down for an hour or two, my eyes would close where I stood. But sleep in this awful place was out of the question. I might well die of exposure. Already my teeth were chattering and I had begun to shiver uncontrollably. Once more I studied the map. Apart from Corrie Etchachan which I'd just climbed, the only way out of the amphitheatre to more sheltered ground appeared to be a gully leading from the northern side of Loch Etchachan down to a deep-sunk ribbon of water — Loch Avon, source of my old acquaintance, the river of the same name. Near the western end of this loch a dot on the map bore the name Shelter Stone. That might be worth investigating.

Skirting the northern shore of Loch Etchachan, I found the gully quite easily and began to scramble down it. There was no path and had it not been for the moon, I would certainly have slipped and might easily have broken an ankle or my neck. I slithered my way down the boulder-choked chasm which at times became so steep that I was forced to turn round and crawl on my belly. By the time I reached the bottom, clouds had obscured the moon and a thick drizzle was falling, although it was not so dark that I couldn't make out my surroundings. I stumbled out of the gully into a surrealist landscape of gigantic boulders. The rain penetrated beneath the cape which I hastily pulled on, and I was soon uncomfortably wet as I picked my way among the enormous stones.

I was trembling with cold and near-exhaustion when I noticed a fantastic boulder looming ahead. It was the size of a cottage and was propped on two smaller stones in such a way as to leave a space beneath. Into this gap I crawled, and switching on my torch, found myself in a narrow passage. This soon widened out into a kind of low but roomy cave beneath the great boulder. The space was absolutely dry and windproof. I could have cried with relief. So this was the Shelter Stone! I pulled on every scrap of clothing I possessed, crawled into my sleeping bag and, pillowing my head on my rucsac, dropped instantly into a profound sleep.

I woke cold, stiff and hungry, but enormously refreshed. For a moment or two I couldn't recall where I was, then memory flooded back, shocking me into instant wakefulness. Light filtered through cracks in the rubble which consolidated the walls of the cave. I struggled out of my sleeping bag, scribbled the date, August 17th, in my notebook then glanced at my watch. I was horrified to see that it was ten o'clock. I stripped off my extra clothing, crammed it with my sleeping bag into my rucsac and crawled out into the open air.

It is impossible to convey the impression of utter desolation which that landscape produced on me. Before me, half-obscured by an icy drizzle, stretched Loch Avon — a lead-coloured ribbon hemmed in an all sides by stark and towering cliffs. The scene looked like a backdrop for some grim Wagnerian drama.

A silver flower bloomed suddenly beside me on the Shelter Stone a split second before the gunshot rang in my ears. Not thirty yards off,

Docherty, his head bandaged, stepped from behind a boulder. A revolver smoked in his hand. Half a mile behind him, a column of dots crawled along the lochside.

"Dinna fash yersel', English," called Docherty, holstering his revolver. He gave his horrible, mad giggle. "Yon wis jist a warnin'. Ah'm comin' tae get ye wi' this," and he flicked open a cut-throat razor. I ducked as something came spinning through the air to land at my feet. I picked it up. It was a sheath knife — my own Bowie.

Docherty put a hand over his eyes. "Ah'm coontin' tae a hunner', English," he called. "Then Ah'm comin'. Yin... twa... three... fower..."

I had no choice but to join in Docherty's hideous game of hide and seek. The blow on the head I had given him must have really sent him over the edge, I thought dully. I forced myself to shake off the numb despair that had gripped me and looked wildly round at the encircling crags. At first glance they looked unclimbable. Then I noticed on the far side of the valley, opposite me, a furrow scored by a stream which cascaded down the near-vertical face. It looked as if it might go, as climbers say.

"... saxteen... seeventeen..."

As I stumbled off through the boulder field, a sullen anger began to replace my physical fear of Docherty. So I was to be mouse to Docherty's cat, was I? He thought I was such easy meat as to return me my knife, did he? I swore to myself I'd make him wish he hadn't, in the event of his closing with me. After his humiliation at my hands the previous evening, he would be obsessed with the need for personal revenge. This crazy duel was his means of reinstating himself in his own eyes and, I suppose, mine. Thank God I'd left the cave beneath the Shelter Stone when I did. The thought of confronting him in that enclosed space sent a shudder through me.

The climb up the side of the stream was desperately hard work but, apart from one or two places where I could have slipped on wet rocks, not particularly dangerous. After about twenty minutes I was forced to stop for a breather. Looking back down the slope, I was surprised at the distance I had climbed. Loch Avon, sunk in its trough of cliffs, was already far below me. The line of dots had turned the head of the loch and was beginning to form a cordon along the base of the slopes beneath. Of Docherty there was no sign, although I was fairly sure he must be coming after me by the route I'd taken — there appeared to be no other gap in the wall of cliffs.

I pressed on. The going was becoming extremely steep, and sheer crags closed in on either side so that I was forced to continue climbing in the stream itself. There followed a short but hair-raising passage over slippery, near-vertical rock steps in the stream bed. Then I climbed through a gap in the crags to find myself on an easier gradient. I thought about waiting there, where I would have Docherty at a disadvantage. Then I realised that this was probably a panic impulse — a desire to bring the conflict to a head and thus end the suspense. I pressed on.

Soon I could see the crest of a long ridge above me. I stopped for another breather and checked the map, confirming that this ridge was in fact the spine connecting Ben Macdui with Cairn Gorm. I allowed myself one minute's rest and was about to set off when I noticed two things which, combined, were to prove my salvation. Firstly, an animal which I associated with Christmas stockings was resting on the slope fifty yards above me. Secondly, a bank of mist was building up along the spine. It appeared that Docherty might have been a bit too clever — if the mist continued to thicken there was a chance of my giving him the slip.

The reindeer did not bolt at my approach, as I had expected it to do, but proceeded to accompany me up the slope. Clearly it was tame, perhaps it hoped I would feed it. A clinking noise caused me to notice a bell hanging round its neck. The mist rolled down to meet us and we plunged into its friendly opaqueness. Up, up, then the ground levelled out beneath my boots and I stood on the crest of the ridge. I flopped down to regain my breath — and as well I did so. A corridor suddenly opened in the mist to reveal for a few moments a fearful precipice a few feet in front of me. Then swirling whiteness filled the gap once more. I looked at Rudolf — folded up beside me like a small grey camel — and an idea suddenly flashed into my head. *I* knew that the reindeer was tame, but did Docherty? Could I use Rudolf as a decoy? It was worth a chance. I cut the bell from Rudolf's neck, crouched behind a nearby boulder and settled down to wait, facing the way Docherty would come if he had followed my route.

My sweat-soaked clothing chilled, but I was too tense to notice the discomfort much. My palms began to sweat and I experienced a hollow, fluttering feeling in my stomach. I looked at the knife in my hand and wondered if I could actually stick the thing into another man in cold blood. Wielding it in self-defence when a native comes at you with an enormous spear, which I may have mentioned is what once happened to me, is another matter. Seconds lengthened into minutes. I began to relax, thinking that perhaps after all I had eluded Docherty in the fog.

Then Rudolf's ears began to flick and he raised his long, serpentine head. A few seconds later I heard the scrape of boots on rock. My stomach tightened and I experienced a coppery taste of fear in my mouth. The sound gradually grew more distinct and suddenly a shadowy form materialised out of the mist about ten yards down the slope. Docherty froze on seeing Rudolf then, realising it wasn't a man, pressed on.

Rudolf wasn't supposed to be tame, so, reaching from behind my boulder, I jabbed him with the knife. With an indignant snort he unfolded himself and loped off into the mist. Docherty topped the slope and halted only a foot or so from my boulder. From his relaxed stance it was clear that my ruse was succeeding, that Rudolf's behaviour had made him think he was along in the vicinity.

My heart had begun to thump wildly and I blinked to clear a mist that seemed to form in front of my eyes. I knew that I must take my chance now, before Docherty turned and spotted me. With a feeling that the whole situation was unreal, I sprang from behind the boulder.

As I crashed into Docherty, my knife-hand drove at his side but the blade turned on something — a buckle or a button. We hit the ground together and I stabbed again. But Docherty was recovering from his surprise with amazing speed and rolled clear. As we scrambled to our feet to face each other, Docherty whipped out his cut-throat razor and flicked it open. A dreamy expression came into his eyes.

"Yon wis naughty, English," he giggled. "Ah'm gaun tae enjoy this."

With a feeling of sick despair, I knew the game was lost. This was obviously the sort of contest in which Docherty excelled. Knowing it was hopeless, I charged at him but he weaved out of the way with an agility that showed me he was master of the situation. I advanced towards him again, but more slowly this time. Step by step he gave ground, the grin on his huge face showing that he was playing with me.

Suddenly, he seemed to lean backwards. An expression of terror wiped the leer from his features, and his arms flailed as he vanished slowly into the mist. A long, diminishing scream came up from below, then a series of muffled thuds, then silence.

10

The Eternal Snows

REACTION SWEPT over me. Sick and trembling, I sat on a boulder. I felt incapable of further effort. Physically, I was very low — my teeth were chattering with cold and my legs ached. The right Achilles tendon was swollen and painful to the touch. Oddly, I didn't feel hungry any more though I was extremely thirsty and probably a bit light-headed too. I found myself thinking of Rachel; pictures floated into my mind — of the two of us striding over the Pentlands, of her flashing pencil recording Grimble's speech in the Chamber, and also of her sailing into battle with Maclean at McKendrick's.

I could have gone on sitting and sitting, and have sunk gradually into a torpor of cold and lethargy. But one part of my brain remained clear, insisting that I study the map and make plans. Feeling as if I were obeying someone else's instructions, I checked my position. It appeared I was on a part of the ridge called Cairn Lochan whose north face was a series of precipices. To the north-east the ridge led to Cairn Gorm, two miles off. To the south it followed a snaking route for three or four miles to the summit of Ben Macdui. I could see no future in heading for Cairn Gorm. In that direction the ridge formed a long peninsula which the soldiers I'd seen earlier would be in the process of cordoning off. I decided to follow the ridge west and south, cross the great trough of the Lairig Ghru and head into the broken country beyond.

I picked up my rucsac and began to move along the ridge, glancing anxiously to my right in case another precipice were suddenly to yawn at my feet. I hadn't gone far when a clatter of stones accompanied by an oath sounded in the mist ahead. Whoever it was, a few more steps would have taken us into each other's radius of visibility. This woke me up with a jolt. I scrambled down off the ridge, to avoid the cordon that must be approaching along its crest, and began to descend in the general direction of Loch Avon.

A barely perceptible difference in the texture of the mist ahead of me sent a warning bell shrilling in my brain. Slowing down, I sensed rather than saw the airy gulf opening in front. I threw a stone. It vanished into the mist and I never heard the sound of its landing. In a kind of despairing fury I staggered round the perimeter of a ring of cliffs which I guessed from the map to be the ones guarding the western approaches to Loch Avon. Once or twice the vapour wreaths parted to disclose harrowing glimpses of sheer rock faces.

All at once I knew that I couldn't go on much longer without rest. And to rest in these wet and cold conditions would merely speed up my physical deterioration. I scanned the map for a red cross which would denote a mountain shelter. Yes, there was one, under a mile to the north-east if my map-reading was correct. All I had to do was to retrace my route along the cliffs and keep following them round until I reached the hut. This route would take me across the stream I'd followed when fleeing from Docherty.

To my vast relief the hut showed up dead on target. It was a tiny affair built of sandbags supported on a frame. A plaque at the entrance announced that this was the reconstructed St. Valery Hut. It was an unspeakable joy to be in out of the cold and the wet. Shivering violently, I stripped off my sodden clothing and changed into fresh underclothes from my rucsac, that were by comparison only slightly damp. I pulled on a spare jersey then donned my outer garments again. After this change of clothing I felt a new man, warm, dry and comfortable — almost. I slowly chewed two Macvita biscuits while I fought off the temptation to fall asleep. With Republican soldiers so thick in the area it would be unwise to stay more than a short while.

I worked out a series of compass bearings on the map to take me over the shoulder of Ben Macdui to the edge of the Lairig pass, going across country instead of along the ridge. Then I crawled reluctantly out of the hut into the grim reality of mist, cold and danger. None too soon — the mist was thinning and visibility had extended to about fifty yards.

Navigating blind through the mist is very much an exercise in faith. There were some nasty moments traversing eternal snowbeds as steep-pitched as a roof and with a glass-like crust. Elsewhere the going was vile: an ankle-jarring scramble over boulder-scree for the most part, though there were occasional patches of sand and gravel.

To my relief I made an accurate landfall — a cluster of tiny lochans. I was now above the cliffs ringing the western end of Loch Etchachan.

Sleet began to replace mist as I toiled up a steep valley leading to the summit-plateau of Ben Macdui. During a pause for rest I glanced at my watch and was amazed to see that it was only three o'clock — five hours since I had left the Shelter Stone that morning.

Once more cold and exhaustion were beginning to sap my reserves. Sleet drove through the neck-opening of my cape. My hands grew numb and blue with cold and my right Achilles tendon now ached continuously. All around me a lunar world of bare boulders and sand was emerging from the mist. The terrain levelled out into a gravelly plateau and I glimpsed the triangulation pillar on Ben Macdui's summit away to my right. White flecks began to drift past me — snow, I realised with a shock. Dear God, snow in August!

A little later I was over the shoulder of the second highest mountain in Britain and looking across the chasm of the Lairig Ghru at the vast cone of Cairntoul, sensed rather than seen through the snowstorm.

The next two hours were sheer hell but I barely remember them. The western face of Ben Macdui, down which I had to climb, was extremely steep and covered in boulder scree. Scrambling over the enormous rocks, with the pack-weight tending to throw you off-balance, would have been a stiff test in good weather for a fit man. For myself, exhausted, soaked, hungry, blinded by flying snow and with my right ankle throbbing painfully, it was an ordeal I would never wish to repeat.

But at last it was over and I was standing on the floor of the Lairig Ghru — a deep stony cleft with a track of sorts running through it. Through this southern end of the pass flowed the Dee, already a fair-sized stream a few miles from its source. I had descended two thousand feet and the snow had given place to a cold rain. I looked downstream for the refuge hut marked on the map as Corrour Bothy. Yes, there it was, a tiny cube a mile distant. The sight was immensely comforting. My body screamed out for rest and also for immediate shelter from the cold that seemed to be seeping into my bones. But before I had taken a step in the direction of the bothy, a line of dots trickled from the hut like dice from a shaker.

It was almost too much. I nearly broke into sobs of frustration. I felt like giving up, but some mad compulsion drove me on. With a feeling of hopeless desperation I began to slog away from the hut up the track, which was more an obstacle course of boulders and pits of sticky peat than a path. Had the soldiers seen me? Even if they hadn't, they must close with me eventually. I was doing my best pace but I couldn't hope to outdistance men who were probably fresh, fit and well-fed.

As I pressed on upstream the terrain to my left began to fall away, gradually disclosing the mouth of a monstrous corrie, over a mile across at its mouth and rearing up two thousand feet in two gigantic steps. Lesser corries gouged its upper slopes. I checked the map. Yes, here it was, the Garrachory — a great bowl-shaped depression between Cairntoul and Braeriach.

I gazed in horror at that stupendous amphitheatre, all spotted with beds of eternal snow and ringed around with grisly precipices. It was like a painting of the Mouth of Hell by Bruegel. And into that mouth I would have to go if I hoped to get clear of the soldiers behind me.

Leaving the path, I swung left into the Garrachory, following the Dee where it came plunging down from the heights. The ground steepened brutally and I was eventually forced to crawl upwards on hands and knees in the rocky trough worn by the narrowing Dee. Slithering on wet rocks, soaked by the icy stream and the icy rain, lungs racked and shoulders aching from the packweight, I struggled up and up more through willpower than by any strength remaining in my trembling limbs.

I reached a confluence and, following the main stream to the right, struggled up and over the first of the corrie's steps. Then I collapsed, utterly spent. I looked down into the gigantic bowl below me but there was no sign of the soldiers. I dared not rest too long, though, as I was shivering violently with cold and knew that my impetus to keep going was running out. I glanced above me at a near-vertical face topped by cliffs. The narrow fissure containing the infant Dee was the only way up. Somehow, I found myself moving upwards once more. It was as though my muscles were functioning by reflex action. Beds of snow moved slowly by. I passed a wondrous thing — an arch of eternal snow spanning the stream. My mind must have wandered a bit for I paused, I cannot remember for how long, to marvel at that bridge to nowhere in a world of barren rock. Then there were no more cliffs above me. just sky and a flat summit plateau and the hump of Braeriach lifting on my right.

I flopped down on the level ground. Looking round I saw that I was on a huge semi-circular ridge studded with tops, the highest of which were Braeriach and Cairntoul. There was no question now of my pressing on to the west as I'd planned earlier. I sensed that unless I could reach shelter fairly soon I was done for. The dreaded cold-wet spiral had caught up with me at last. This means that if you get beyond a certain stage of exhaustion, in exposed conditions and wearing wet clothing, your body heat simply begins to leak away even if you keep moving. You start shivering, which uses up energy, which uses up heat, and unless broken the spiral culminates eventually in death. It was no longer raining but, what was worse, a biting wind was roaring across the ridge, bringing about the same effect as a drastic fall in temperature.

I scanned the map for a mountain refuge and saw there was one four or five miles to the north, the Sinclair Memorial Hut, at the north end of the Lairig Ghru. To reach it, I must follow the summit ridge round over Braeriach till it intersected the Lairig's western wall, then walk along above the pass till I reached the hut.

I was weaving like a drunk man when I set off. Fortunately it was still light enough to see clearly and all I had to do to reach my destination was to follow the lip of the Lairig, then cut down. To have worked out and navigated a compass course would have been beyond my powers at that stage. I can remember little of the final instalment of my day's journeying except that I nearly blundered over cliffs on Braeriach's south face, and that I whistled continuously 'The Haughs o' Cromdale' and the other tunes remembered from The Two Geordies, in order to keep my mind functioning at a conscious level. All around it gradually became dark. It was past midnight when I finally reached the north end of the Lairig and began stumbling down the slope in what I hoped was the direction of the Sinclair Hut.

However, in the darkness and in my dazed and exhausted state, I must have overshot the hut. I stumbled down the slope till I reached the floor of the Lairig. A fit man could have easily cast about till he located the Sinclair. But I knew all at once that I lacked the strength to climb only a short way back up the slope, even if my life depended on it. I cursed myself with incredible venom — perhaps it was the only way to prevent a fatal descent into total stupor.

More by instinct than by any reasoning that it would lead me to lower and less exposed terrain, I plodded downhill beside the stream that flowed out of the northern mouth of the pass. I had stumbled along for perhaps a mile when, raising my head, I saw to my inexpressible relief a light shining some distance in front of me.

A little later I was knocking on the porchway door of a building that seemed to be built of logs in Swiss chalet style. An electric light burning in the porch had attracted my attention. I remember running my fingers over the wood to check that I wasn't imagining it all.

Suddenly a window lit up beside the porch and the door opened, revealing a tall, lantern-jawed man with high cheekbones on which sprouted tufts of hair. He took one look at me, then his arm was round my shoulders and he was helping me inside. I was guided into a large, comfortable room, all pine panelling and stonework, with a bar at one end and climbers' helmets, ice-axes and other mountaineering items decorating the walls.

"Now chust you sit down," a voice said solicitously in the soft, lilting sing-song which suggested origins well to the west of Spey. "I'll fetch plankets and get the fire going whateffer. But first you must pe changing those wet clothes." Then he muttered with some preoccupation, "Shew mercy and compassion every man unto his brother, Zechariah 7, verse 9."

11

The Tin Dragonfly

TWENTY MINUTES LATER, clad in pyjamas under an ancient tweed suit, cocooned in blankets and ensconced in a deep armchair before a crackling wood fire, I was trying to regain sufficient sense of coordination to sup a delicious broth. A warm glow was beginning to spread through my body, driving out the chill and exhaustion from my bones.

"You're very kind," I mumbled to my host who beamed at me from the other side of the fire. "Fraid I got lost in the hills." My brain baulked at the task of a more detailed explanation.

"Och, these hills iss the te-e-erriple things whateffer. Lucky it wass for you, you saw my light. That iss why I keep it purning — ass a guide to penighted hill-walkers. Behold, I am against thee, O destroying mountain, saith the Lord, Jeremiah 51, verse 25." He waved at the climbing gear on the walls. "All the hikers and climbing poys know Uncle Shamus of the Rothiemurchus Inn."

While I spooned up my broth, Uncle Shamus chatted away about the Cairngorms and their lore — mountaineers past and present, acts of climbing folly or heroism, local characters from the communities round the great massif's perimeter and some story about a Grey Man, liberally sprinkling his anecdotes with scriptural tags. I got the impression of a garrulous, sociable man who knew everybody and everything in his parish.

Before I had finished my soup I was starting to nod.

"Och, what am I thinking off!" declared Uncle Shamus, noticing. "Here haff I been running on and you a sick man. What have I done unto thee? and wherein have I wearied thee? Micah 6, verse 3. Bed it iss for you."

He helped me into a small bedroom at the back of the building. The sensation of sliding between the sheets was purest bliss. Within seconds of my head touching the pillow I was asleep.

I woke, feeling marvellously clear-headed and physically refreshed. Sunlight was pouring through a window. The events of the previous day began to filter back into my memory and suddenly alarm bells were shrilling in my brain. The Agreement! I threw back the sheets intending to inspect the contents of my rucsac to see if anything was missing. But then there came a tap on the door and Uncle Shamus entered with all my clothes, which he laid carefully on a chair.

He enquired how I had slept, pressed me to stay for as long as I wanted, brushed aside offers of payment and generally showered me with solicitations.

But I was no longer the shattered wreck of the night before to whom comforting words brought reassurance as to a child. Uncle Shamus' black eyes, twinkling above those enormous cheek-bones, had seemed last night to reflect sagacity and concern; now they seemed merely calculating. The smiling mouth which, framed by those lantern jaws, had appeared so good-humoured now seemed set in a false and crafty grin. I felt rather like the grandmother in the tale of Red Riding Hood. Uncle Shamus might or might not be just a gossipy old innkeeper with a penchant for quoting scripture; I wasn't taking any chances on it, though.

He proceeded to ply me with questions, skilfully wrapped up inside a smokescreen of polite enquiries and apparent concern on my behalf. How far had I travelled? Where from? Where to? Why? Had I met up with troops? Had I contacted anyone? What were my plans now? To all these queries I returned vague or ambiguous replies, pretending to be still too exhausted to answer in more detail, and presently he abandoned his interrogation.

Uncle Shamus raised his hands protestingly when I asked if I could stay another night. "Och, chust you stay ass long ass you like. You iss not to think off going until you iss fully recovered whateffer. O Lord, so wilt thou recover me, and make me to live, Isaiah 38, verse 16."

A few minutes later, he brought me a meal on a tray. When he returned for the tray I was apparently in a profound slumber.

Soon after, I heard the put-put of a moped engine. I clambered stiffly out of bed and, looking through the window, saw Uncle Shamus puttering away down an unmetalled road that led towards a sheet of water enclosed by pine forests. Beyond the trees the land dropped away to a broad river valley with roads and settlements. Speyside, I supposed.

I tore open my rucsac. Thank God the Agreement was still there. As I dressed, my brain worked overtime. Glancing at my watch, I saw that it was four in the afternoon. My request to remain at the inn may have bought me a little time but I couldn't rely on it. At any moment the innkeeper might bring the soldiers about my ears, so I had to be on my way — fast. I studied my map with furious concentration. By heading south through the Lairig Ghru then following the Dee I would come eventually to an unmetalled road where a bridge carried it across the river. The road followed the Dee eastwards, joining up with a metalled road that led to Braemar. Rachel's country cottage was near Braemar. If she could meet me in her car at the bridge...

I hobbled through the lounge and dialled Rachel's number from a phone behind the bar. It suddenly struck me that I was apparently alone in the inn, which seemed odd when the climbing season still had a few weeks to run.

I sagged with relief when she answered.

"It's Nick, Rachel. Look, I can't explain now but I'm in bad trouble and I need your help." I explained my plan to rendezvous at the bridge over the Dee. "I ought to make it by the early hours of the morning, so you'd better be there at midnight."

She didn't argue or ask questions, just said she'd be there. It seemed that we still needed each other.

As I replaced the phone I noticed something gleaming on a shelf under the bar. With a growing certainty that my suspicions were to be confirmed, I bent down to look, and discovered a loaded revolver. A strange article for a peaceful innkeeper to keep handy!

My need is greater than thine, I misquoted to myself as I stuffed the revolver into my rucsac. I arranged a pillow inside my bed so that at a casual glance it looked as if it had a sleeping occupant. I buckled on my Bowie, slung my map-case round my neck and eased on my rucsac. Then I slipped out of the inn and headed for the great V of the Lairig's mouth. There, plain as a pikestaff, was the Sinclair Hut, perched halfway up the western arm.

I was taking a desperate gamble, but I couldn't see any better alternative. In fact, to plunge back into the very area where I'd nearly been caught was on the face of its so crazily perverse that it just might come off.

Fringed with cliffs, the walls of the defile closed in. Soon the path disappeared under a litter of boulder scree which involved arduous scrambling. Losing my stiffness, I reached the summit and stepped round two tiny lochans beyond which the pass began to open out.

Presently the Garrachory yawned, stark and ghastly to my right, and the Dee rushed down to march with the path. I came level with the hut where I'd seen the soldiers, then, after passing the huge pinnacle of the Devil's Point, I came out of the Lairig as the evening shadows began to flow up its slopes.

With the Cairngorms now behind me, I pressed on in the gathering darkness over a stretch of undulating heathery country where four glens met, then plunged into Glen Dee, hemmed in by high mountains. The path now degenerated into a slough of gritty porridge composed of peat and crumbled granite. This was to prove my undoing: without warning my right leg sank to the knee in a sludge-filled hole and I fell heavily, thrown off balance by the packweight. An excruciating pain shot through my ankle as I pulled my leg free. I examined the ankle and decided that, though not broken, it was badly sprained.

I removed Uncle Shamus' revolver and the Agreement from my rucsac and stuffed it in my belt along with the revolver. Then I hobbled on my way, after weighting the rucsac with stones and sinking it in the Dee. I could now only move at a lurching shuffle. It was impossible entirely to keep the weight off my injured ankle and the pain was so great that I had to make frequent halts to ease it. Once, when I tripped, the agony was so intense that I passed out momentarily.

I managed to make steady, if terribly slow progress and, when the first light began to sweep down the widening walls of the glen, I reckoned I couldn't be far from the rendezvous. Coming round a shoulder of hillside I saw below me a great rock-girt pool — the Chest of Dee, and a quarter of a mile beyond it, a substantial bridge spanning the river on stone piers.

But there was no sign of any car.

Despair washed over me as I stumbled down the path. Rachel must have changed her mind about coming: since our quarrel it would need a compelling reason to bring her to my assistance. For all she knew, my trouble might be purely personal — Perhaps I was on the run after beating up a soldier. She probably thought I was a thoroughly bad lot after the performance last time we were together. In effect, I began to feel very sorry for myself.

All at once I became aware of a distant noise. I stopped to listen. The sound grew rapidly louder and in a few moments I recognised the clattering roar of a helicopter engine. Wildly I glanced round for cover, but in that steep, bare place I was as exposed and helpless as a beetle in a bathtub.

The shining perspex bubble of the helicopter's dome floated above the lip of the far side of the glen. The machine whirled over me like a monstrous metal insect, turned in a swinging side-slipping movement and circled for a bombing run.

I flung myself behind a boulder as a line of earth fountains raced towards me; the rattle of machine-gun fire cut through the engine's clattering morse. Bullets smacked and spanged against the rock while I tried desperately to contract my shrinking body into the tightest possible ball. Then the hellish din of the machine gun cut out as the helicopter swept over me.

I couldn't stay where I was — the boulder was small and tilted in such a way as to give protection only from the front. About twenty yards to my left a much larger boulder offered far better protection. Fighting down the paralyzing fear that threatened to glue me to my present spot, I launched myself towards it at the same instant noticing from the corner of my eye the helicoper banking for another attack. So intense was my concentration on reaching safety that I was hardly aware of the racket of the machine gun as I stumbled across the intervening space. I had almost reached my objective when a giant invisible hand seemed to pick me up and fling me sideways. Then I had reached the boulder and rolled behind it just as the helicopter roared over me.

As I yanked Uncle Shamus' revolver from my belt, I noticed with detached surprise blood welling from my side: no time to attend to that now. Peeping round the edge of my shelter, I saw the helicopter hovering, choosing the direction for its next run-in. I observed that the cabin contained one other man beside the pilot.

I studied the revolver closely for the first time. It was to be my sole weapon in a ridiculously one-sided duel. It was one that I was familiar with, a .38 Army model — a good handgun, packing plenty of punch yet not so heavy as to make really accurate aim impossible, bearing in mind that any revolver is accurate only within a limited range.

So it was with some confidence in my ability to handle the weapon — though with little in the outcome of the contest — that I showed myself round the side of the boulder to draw the enemy. The helicopter came at me immediately, machine gun stuttering. I withdrew behind the rock then, when the thrashing of the rotor sounded almost overhead, forced myself, sweating and sick with fright, to move out into the open. The thing seemed to be almost on top of me, filling my whole field of vision. Stone chips from machine gun bullets sprayed up in front of me as I took aim at the pilot, and I felt an angry tug at my anorak sleeve. Then I was suddenly icy cool and my hand was perfectly steady as I squeezed the trigger.

The helicopter swept over my head. I swivelled round to await its next charge. To my amazement I saw it dip sharply forward and begin to spin on its own axis, like a sycamore seed twirling to earth. Now was my chance, before the second man could take over the controls. I hobbled forward and began to blaze away at the perspex bubble. The other man was reaching over the slumped body of the pilot.

One of my bullets must, I think, have struck some part of the tail rotor, for a loud clang sounded above the thrashing of the engine and the machine lurched violently then fluttered down towards the river. Fascinated, I watched the thing swoop about in demented circles like a drunken dragonfly and finally corkscrew into the rocks above the Chest of Dee, where it blossomed into an enormous orange flower. A pall of smoke was roiled upwards as the explosion hit my ears.

I tossed the empty revolver into the Dee and stumbled on my way. I was beginning to tremble with reaction. A dull ache in my side reminded me that I had been hit. I looked down and felt sick and faint. A dark-red patch was spreading on the side of my anorak. I sat down and located the wound — a hole in my side I could put two fingers in. I stuffed half my handkerchief into the wound and with shaking fingers tore my vest into strips. I knotted the strips together and bound the wad into place.

I must have passed out soon afterwards, for the next thing I knew about was opening my eyes and seeing very vividly Rachel's face above me with tears streaming down her cheeks.

12
Tea and Sympathy

WHEN I CAME TO again I was in bed in a neat cheerful little room with lines of books on shelves and vases full of flowers. I felt extremely weak, but at the same time possessed of the heightened perception which sometimes comes after illness. For a minute or two I was disorientated, then disconnected bits of the past began to surface in my memory and assemble themselves like the pieces of a jigsaw, until I could recall everything up to the moment of my entering the house. Had I really seen Rachel or was I dreaming? That was, let me see — August 19th. I put a hand to my face and felt luxuriant stubble. God, I must have been here for days!

The realisation sent adrenalin coursing through my blood. I pushed back the bedclothes — noticing that I was wearing pyjamas, something I normally never do — and swung my feet onto the floor. I stood up, or tried to, and found myself sprawling on the floor. The door opened and in swept Rachel, looking smart and capable in blue denim shirt and jeans.

"I'm okay, Rachel," I reassured her as she helped me back into bed. "I feel fine — just a bit off-colour, that's all." Then I burst into tears of relief.

She propped me up in bed and fed me soup. With each spoonful I felt my strength returning. She cleared away the tray then came back and sat on my bed. I took her hand and a companionable silence grew between us.

"Friends?" I asked at length, a little diffidently.

"Of course." She smiled warmly and squeezed my hand. "I'm sorry I was so beastly to you on the journey up. I didn't really mean the things I said."

"When I didn't see your car at the bridge I thought you'd decided not to come. Thank God I was wrong."

"I hid the car under the bridge. I didn't want it spotted by the military."

"How did you know I was in *that* sort of trouble?" I asked in surprise. "I didn't give any details on the phone."

"It wasn't too difficult to guess. Things have been hotting up since I saw you last. For example, there are some blood-curdling stories going around about the 'reconstruction' of the Shetlanders. Seems Maclean's behind it. He's really spreading his wings these days. Apparently he runs some sort of Commando training school on an island in the Forth."

"Another thing — you've got to be careful what you say. An artist friend of mine was blacked the other day, and the paper he works for rapped over the knuckles, for bringing out a cartoon showing Maclean as Napoleon, the boss-pig in *Animal Farm*. So when you said you were in trouble, knowing your tactful retiring disposition, I thought it highly possible you'd trodden on some official toes. Seems I was right. They must have been pretty cross to set a chopper on you."

"Listen, Rachel, there's something you have to know," I said, when she'd cleared away the tray. Then I told her everything — what I'd overheard at the house near Tomintoul and about my subsequent movements.

I don't quite know what I expected her reaction to be — shock or consternation, perhaps even delight at stumbling on a story that would have the world by its ears. Instead, she gave me a look of tender concern and murmured, "Poor old Nick. You've certainly been through it. Sorting your things out, I came across a document in code — obviously the Agreement you've just been telling me about. Don't worry — I packed it away in a drawer with the rest of your stuff, even though I was dying to know what it said." Then she became coolly analytical. "Actually, I'm not really surprised that things have gone the way they have. I've always thought it was on the cards that the Freedom Party might take an extreme stand if pressed hard enough, but there's a chance it wouldn't stop there."

"How do you mean?"

"Maclean makes no secret of his hopes to become the architect of a Pan-Celtic League, a socialist confederation of communities with Celtic ties or affinities — Scotland, Wales, Ireland, France, Spain, Portugal, Quebec Province, Nova Scotia and some of the Irish-American groups."

"Oh — come on. That's a bit far-fetched, surely?"

"I know — 'It couldn't happen here'," rejoined Rachel tartly. "Well, just consider the facts. Welsh nationalism's taken a militantly leftish turn. Anything could happen in Ireland now that there's full-scale civil war. In France that big corruption scandal among top Ministers last year nearly swept the Communists into power. In Spain the Communists are making a determined bid for power, and they're coming back fighting in Portugal. In North America Québec Libre, Sinn Feinn and Mic an Froaich — that means 'Sons of the Heather', a Gaelic-speaking separatist movement in Nova Scotia — are going from strength to strength, probably with powerful Communist backing. The material's there — all that's needed is a man with enough force and vision to shape it to his purpose. And who's to say Maclean's not such a man?"

"A Communist Atlantic Alliance," I mused aloud. "It doesn't bear thinking about."

Rachel's face had taken on a characteristic expression of absorbed concentration.

"Now — about getting you to the Border, Nick." No weighing up of risks, no consideration about whether or not to get involved, just an immediate, total commitment to helping a friend in need. No doubt she also felt that politically it was her duty to assist me, but I think it was personal loyalty that counted most.

A rush of gratefulness swept over me. "Thanks," I muttered, inadequately. "By the way, how long have I been here?"

"Let's see. Today's the 25th — that's six days. No, Nick, you stay put! You'd lost a lot of blood and developed a fever. You've been delirious most of the time. You were lucky — that bullet pierced the abdominal wall only and didn't hit any organ. The wound's healing nicely. The fever broke last night."

Six days! That meant that I had barely a fortnight to complete my mission.

"Good God, Rachel — the balloon goes up on September 11th! I'll have to leave here at once."

"And how far do you think you'd get, Nick?" asked Rachel, shaking her head. "A few minutes ago you weren't even able to get back into bed on your own." She frowned slightly and went on after a pause, "I think I know how it can be managed. We must allow an absolute minimum of four days for you to recuperate. Then I'll take you in my car to the Border. There are places you can slip across on foot without being caught."

"But suppose we're stopped. By now I must be the most wanted man in Scotland. I'd be recognised straight away."

"I don't think so, Nick," said Rachel looking at me in an appraising way. "Will you trust me to fix things?"

I woke again six hours later. Rachel fed me more soup and filled me in on some details. Her cottage was a converted shooting lodge a few miles south of Braemar and approached from the A93 by an unmetalled track impassable to any vehicle except a Land Rover. Here at weekends and vacations she could relax, write magazine articles and practise archery — a sport it transpired, at which she was highly proficient. Then she unfolded the plan that she had devised to get me south and across the Border.

Thanks to Rachel's nursing and my tough constitution, I made a rapid recovery. The peace of that lonely spot, where the only living creatures besides ourselves were great golden eagles, was balm to my soul. Some kindly alchemy of Nature had transmuted the place into a green cup with limpid, fern-lined pools, starred with tiny, bright flowers — a strange contrast to the bare mountains all around. I have come across such spots only a few times in my life — in the northern Serengeti, in the Ruwenzori foothills, in Kenya's Aberdare range. The common factor in my experience has always been what I can only describe as a sort of charged serenity. If I were superstitious I would believe that such places were the abodes of good and happy spirits.

Soon I was up and about and, to help get my strength back, took up archery under Rachel's exacting guidance. I blasted away by the hour at target faces fixed to a butt of straw bales, using tubular aluminium arrows and a bow of wood and laminated fibreglass. I got the hang of the game quickly and was soon grouping my arrows at forty yards, which Rachel grudgingly admitted wasn't bad for a beginner.

Fever and loss of blood had left me feeling weak as a kitten on my recovering consciousness, so that initially I was utterly dependent on Rachel. I chafed secretly a good deal over this at first, but her selfless dedication and surprisingly obvious pleasure in nursing me gradually melted my resentment. There was nothing else to be done for it.

In the evenings, as part of the preparation for the escape plan, we had long talks in Swahili concerning the rise of a certain Kariuki from herdboy on a Kenya farm to research student, via Mission School and Makerere College.

I gave myself a final rinse then tipped the water from the hip bath out of the back door. The water now owed its brownish discolouration to peat and rusty pipes and no longer to stain; the towel showed no trace of brown after I'd dried myself. I shaved the back of my hands, then rubbed stain-remover into my palms and soles until they changed from a dark chocolate colour to muddy pink.

Now for the bit I dreaded. I removed a pair of tinted contact lenses from their case. These were cosmetic lenses, whose function was to alter the colour of the eyes, not to correct vision. They were apparently mostly worn by girls at parties, for fun. I moistened the lenses with a special wetting fluid. Then, flinching and blinking, I positioned each lens with a forefinger on the cornea over the pupil. After a few seconds my eyes stopped running.

I changed the dressing on my wound, which was knitting up nicely. Then, feeling rather self-conscious, I wrapped the towel round my middle and called to Rachel that I was ready.

She opened the kitchen door, stopped dead and clapped her hands. Her eyes widened.

"Eeeeeh, mzuri sana — mzuri mingi sana!" she giggled imitating the sycophantic cackle of a tribal wife. Then more seriously "That's really great. And now — the final touch."

I sat down and she rubbed some adhesive onto my shaven head. As she stood beside me, her supple fingers working over my scalp, I became keenly aware of her physical proximity. Her firmly rounded breasts were only inches from my face. An exciting smell of skin and scent stirred my senses. Then she picked up the wig she'd made from black-dyed sheep's wool and moulded it to my scalp. Stepping back to assess the result, she smiled and nodded her head vigorously. Eyes shining, she led me into her room to look at myself in her wardrobe mirror.

The black stranger who stared back at me from the glass with eyes that were both brown, instead of one blue and the other grey, bore no resemblance to Nicholas Wainwright. It was astonishing, even disturbing — as though I had somehow lost my own body and found myself reincarnated as a negro. For the figure in the glass that mimicked my movements *was* a negro — slightly diluted perhaps with a dash of Somali or Arab blood as the thin features hinted, but undeniably a negro. The slim girl standing beside him could easily have been his sister.

I was suddenly aware of a charged feeling between us, a feeling sparked off by my new identity. Rachel jerked at the towel round my middle and the African in the mirror was suddenly naked.

"There!" she muttered fiercely.

A mad excitement surged through me. I turned to face her and saw my desire mirrored in her eyes.

"I don't think we should have done that, Kariuki," she murmured contentedly, some time later. She traced a pattern with her finger on my strange new black skin. "Your're supposed to be convalescing."

Nicholas Wainwright had vanished, totally and without trace. His place had been taken by Kariuki, Rachel's cousin, like herself a Kikuyu. We would drive as close to the Border as we could without attracting the attention of frontier patrols. Then I would slip across under cover of night. This last seemed to me the only risky part for I reckoned that my negro disguise should guarantee total security.

In order to act the part of Kariuki convincingly I had put into practice a theory of disguise which an old Kenya settler of Boer descent had once explained to me. Atmosphere was the great thing, the old Afrikaner had insisted. Merely changing your appearance wasn't enough — you had to think yourself into the part until you *were* it. Accordingly, I had sunk myself in the role so thoroughly that I could identify with the character without conscious effort. We were due to leave early next morning. The one tiny flaw in my cover was my lack of Kikuyu. But I thought the chances of running into someone who could tell that we were speaking Swahili rather than Kikuyu were pretty negligible.

During a long, deliciously langorous afternoon made cosier by the patter of rain on the windows we chatted quietly, had a real Scottish tea with scones and various kinds of teabread, then made love again, prolonged, gentle love this time. As darkness began to gather in the room, we drifted off to sleep in each other's arms.

I was wakened by the roar of a vehicle approaching the house. Headlights suddenly shone into the room. The vehicle pulled up, car doors slammed, boots thudded, and voices rang out. Seconds later a knocking shook the front door.

Rachel had assessed the situation and decided how to meet it while I was still gathering my wits.

"Car keys," she snapped, grabbing them from her bedside chair. "Out of the window. I'll try to cover up."

I snatched the keys from her, grabbed my boots, clothes and belt with

Bowie attached, and peered through the half-open window. A soldier stood beside the wall a few yards to the left of the window, submachine gun at the ready. In desperation I grabbed a hairbrush from the dressing-table and hurled it sideways through the window. It clattered against a stone. The soldier, clearly suspicious, started walking towards the source of the sound. While his attention was distracted I scrambled out and pelted off into the darkness. Stones hurt my feet, but I put a hundred yards between myself and the house before stopping to pull on my clothes and boots and to buckle on my Bowie. Then, with presence of mind restored completely, I picked up the track and headed for the main road at my best speed.

13
Cowboys and Indians

AS I RAN I tried to think constructively. It was up to Rachel, if she could, to prevent the Agreement — locked in a drawer when the soldiers arrived — from falling into the hands of the patrol. For my part, I must attempt to cross the Border on my own and try to get the Westminster authorities to listen to me. The chances of either of us succeeding looked, I had to admit, pretty slim. And God knows what would happen to her when they found out I had been at the cottage.

I felt horribly low. If I hadn't allowed my senses to become dulled to the possibility of danger, we wouldn't have been caught off guard. The realisation that I was once again on the run, pursued by an implacable enemy, was beginning to get through, filling me with a kind of despairing horror. I very nearly turned round and went back.

I reached the lay-by where Rachel's car — a small Ford — was parked. Unlocking it, I scrambled in and started the engine. Then tore away, crashing through the gear changes, and roared southwards up Glen Clunie with the pedal rammed onto the floor. I had travelled less than a mile when, topping a rise, I saw oncoming headlights rushing towards me. The approaching car stopped, reversed, then slewed sideways across the road to bar my passage. My headlights showed a Land Rover with two Republican soldiers in the front.

I braked to a screeching halt, wrestled the Ford round and hurtled back down the road in the direction of Braemar. Anyone who has learned to drive on Kenya roads, pot-holed and corrugated in the dry season, sticky morasses in the wet, drives well — not the same thing as driving safely with which it tends to be equated in Britain. I held the car at eighty all the way down the glen, whipping round corners with a scream of brakes and whiff of burning rubber — one particularly sharp dry skid almost taking me right off the road.

An occasional glance to the rear confirmed that I was pulling away fast from my pursuers. But as I whirled through the sleeping village, I realised that I daren't stay on the main road. The pursuit had only to phone ahead from Braemar to have the road sealed off.

I snaked round a huge curve into Deeside, then gunned the car for all she was worth along a level winding stretch of road with the river gleaming below me and a dark cliff of forest looming to my right. At last I saw what I was looking for. Flashing across a bridge over the Dee, I came to where the A93 crossed an unmetalled road. With a screech of tortured tyres, I wrenched the Ford round practically on two wheels, then sped down the right-hand fork. Back over the Dee I raced, then into the friendly gloom of the trees. Though the top was good for a dirt road, I was forced to drop speed as the low-slung Ford could easily have come to grief on the uneven surface. The Land Rover, with its high clearance, would have the edge on me if it got on my trail. I might be able to lose them for good if I could throw off pursuit long enough to get on to a metalled road.

Crashing into potholes and jolting over bumps, I drove as fast as I dared along a maze of forest tracks, passing an occasional cottage and, once, a distillery. Then I burst out onto open moorland. Suddenly a herd of deer galloped in file across the road in front of me. There was no time to take avoiding action and I tensed against the shock of impact, but the beast converging on my car soared into the air, clearing the roof with a rattle of hoofs on steel.

I have a good sense of direction, developed by long safaris in the Kenya bush, and I thought the road was trending southwards away from Deeside, which was all to the good. As I bucketed along for mile after mile over that bare moor, I suddenly became concerned about a rattling behind me, inside the car. Glancing over my soldier, I was relieved to see that the source of the noise was just one of Rachel's bows bouncing about amid a litter of loose arrows.

My relief was short-lived. A wall of forest reared up in front; just before I plunged into it a gleam from distant headlights reflected momentarily in my driving mirror. As the trees closed round me the road ahead forked. Left or right? I swerved right, as this seemed to be the more southerly. After about a mile I left the trees and a little later was careering along beside a loch skirting the roadside to my left. The road entered a stand of firs, passed a stone house, and stopped.

I skidded to a halt, then backed the car off the road into the trees. End of the line. I grabbed a torch from the glove locker and Rachel's bow and a bundle of arrows from the back seat, then scrambled out of the car. The air felt calm and mild. No light or sound came from the house; if it were empty I would, I decided, make a stand there. The building was a compact, solid affair of two storeys, and had that indefinable air of being untenanted.

I tried the front door; it was locked. Then I prowled round the place confirming that it was empty. Had I been less preoccupied, I would have been surprised at the meticulous order and the Looking-Glass atmosphere of the interior disclosed by my torch — lace curtains behind the windows, shiny brass beds neatly made up, massive furniture of oak and mahogany, photographs in silver frames, and plaster statuettes of caber-tossing Highlanders with mutton-chop whiskers. An inscription carved above the front door told me that this was Allt an Dearg Shiel Lodge, built in 1869 by HRH Queen Victoria.

Getting in presented no difficulty, which was just as well. I had to move fast. I simply forced the blade of my Bowie between the upper and lower sashes of one of the windows and eased back the catch. After retracing my steps a little way down the road, I moved backwards to the window, brushing out all the tracks with a fir branch. Then I climbed in, knocking a kilted hammer-thrower onto the floor, and re-latched the window. I found myself in a large study like room with a desk, bookcase, tables and chairs under dustsheets. The door proved to be locked. Flashing my torch under the door, I peered through the keyhole and saw a hallway with a staircase. The decor in the hall was stags' heads and more miniature Gaels. Boots crunching on bits of plaster, I crouched beside the window to await developments.

These were not long in coming. Minutes later the Land Rover pulled up beside the house. Boots clumped round the building. The front door was tried. Presently a humming noise started up from somewhere at the back, an electricity generator by the sound. My pursuers were not going to risk being jumped in the dark.

I had recovered some poise by this time and my mind was beginning to function more or less coolly. The plan, if it can be called that, was simply to let fly with an arrow the moment one or other of my enemies showed up. With a considerable effort I strung Rachel's bow, set the adjustable sight to the bunny, or close-range mark, then placed my arrows within easy reach. They were target arrows with conical piles; for killing a tri-angular steel broadhead is used. But I reckoned that at close range even a target arrow would prove quite lethal. Lacking a bracer, whose function is to gather up loose clothing against fouling the bowstring, I stripped my top half to the vest.

I jumped violently as a burst of automatic fire unlocked the front door.

"We ken ye're there, Wainwright," bellowed a voice. "Gie yersel' up. Ten seconds. Then we're comin' in."

The front door was eventually kicked open and bullets sprayed the hall — doubtless shattering a few more plaster Highlanders. Light appeared under the door of my room. Steps sounded beyond the door, one set in the hallway, the other going upstairs. Checking that the cock feather was pointing outwards, as Rachel had shown me, I nocked one of my arrows onto the bowstring and took up my stance in the corner diagonally opposite the door.

Now for the draw. Feet apart, arms pushing bow and string away from each other till the pile crept up to the arrow-rest, at the same time raising the bow, with the arms and head in the same plane as the legs. Bowstring well into the chin with the knuckle of the drawing hand pressed into the angle of the jaw to give a good anchor, back of the drawing hand flat and in line with the forearm. I fought to control the trembling in my left arm as the tension in the fibreglass struggled for release. Then I came down to half draw to conserve energy.

Another burst of fire roared out. The door juddered and swung open, releasing light into the room. Blinking to adjust my vision, I sensed that the next development would be a gun barrel poking round the doorway, then a blast of bullets.

"Hold it!" I yelled. "I'm coming out."

"Hands on yere heid," called the voice from the other side of the wall. "Come oot real slow."

The next few moments were among the worst in my life. I had heard about the momentarily paralysing effect of a surprise appearance — bank robbers in Mickey Mouse masks, the girl agent who barged naked into the opposition's HQ and gunned them all down while they were still gawping. I tried hard to remember if such things were truth or fiction. Doubtless the theory was sound, but... Despite the enormity of that 'but', I found myself going through the door — bow at full draw — before the dregs of my resolution quite drained away.

Suddenly I was face to face with a tall man holding a submachine gun. In the frozen instant of time that our eyes met, inconsequent details stamped themselves on my awareness — the man's blue chin and heavy eyebrows, a rip in the poncho he was wearing, a fragment of heather caught in the gunsight. The man's eyes widened. Before he could recover from the Robin-Hood-in-blackface apparition confronting him, I had sighted on his chest and released the bowstring.

The man jerked back as though yanked by a rope. A feathered stump suddenly and shockingly appeared in his shoulder. The gun clattered on the floor.

I scooped it up. Then I motioned him into the room I'd come out of and followed him. The bright red shaft sticking out of the back of his shoulder was incredible and disquieting — like a detail in a surrealist painting.

"Tell your pal to come down," I rasped. "No funny business or I'll let you have it."

The soldier's face had turned white with shock and pain. Blood oozed from around the arrow shaft and trickled down his poncho. He gulped, then called in a fairly steady voice, "Ye can come doon noo, MacSween. Ah've got him covered."

"Guid work, corp," shouted his companion from above and clumped downstairs. As he stepped through the doorway, weapon casually pointing at the floor, I moved from behind the door and told him to release his gun.

The soldier, a thickset little man with a freckled face whirled round and stared at me. His jaw and his gun dropped at the same instant. "Christ — a bluidy Spade!" he exclaimed.

I made them stand facing against one wall then hit each of them hard on the back of the head with the gun barrel. They slumped to the floor. I shot open some more doors till I located the kitchen. Hanging from the ceiling was a pulley — a contraption used in traditional Scottish households for airing clothes, consisting of a frame of wooden slats raised and lowered by a miniature block and tackle.

With rope from this device I did a very thorough job of tying up my two pursuers, after removing their ponchos and sidepacks. More investigation of the house disclosed a curious room at the back that put me in mind of a torture chamber of the Inquisition — more blocks and tackle fixed to the ceiling with sharp hooks suspended from ropes. It dawned on me that this was probably the larder for hanging deer carcases. At any event, it was tailor-made for my purpose.

After seeing to the wounded man's shoulder, I dragged the two of them into the larder. After gagging them both, I roped the small one by his belt to one of the hooks, hauled him up to the ceiling and cleated the rope. He wouldn't be able to free himself in a hurry when he came to. The wounded one, I reckoned, was *hors de combat*. They were in for an uncomfortable spell all right, but such were the fortunes of war; their release was only a matter of time. Sooner or later the house would be searched as the hunt got under way.

I ransacked the house for food and clothing, but drawers and cupboards were either empty or contained dreary, inedible things like blankets, linen, mops and pails. However, in one of the soldiers' sidepacks I found an immense, thick jam sandwich. This I demolished in record time. Donning my top clothing and the unperforated poncho, I stuffed Rachel's torch in a pocket. Then, concealing the bow and arrows in a cupboard and bundling the guns under an arm, I switched off the lights and slipped out of the house. Outside it was almost dark. The gun which had been fired I chucked into the loch and slung the other over my shoulder.

When I tried to start up Rachel's car nothing happened. I peered inside the bonnet and discovered that my late pursuers had thoughtfully smashed the distributor head. On the front seat of the Land Rover I found a couple of Ordnance Survey maps covering the area. These I shoved in my anorak map pocket. I was tempted to take the Land Rover, but decided reluctantly that the vehicle was too hot for safety.

I was too weak from my recent wound to contemplate trying to reach the Border on foot, even if I could have made it in time. This was of the essence in more ways than one, for my negro disguise was now a massive disadvantage, eliminating all problems of identification for my pursuers once the soldiers in the shooting lodge had been liberated. I could, I suppose, have gone back and killed them off. But, at the risk of being thought a sentimental reactionary, I believe that a basic code of decency is worth living by even if at times it seems costly and inconvenient.

A moment's consideration and I decided to make for the east coast, which wasn't by my reckoning too distant, then try to stow away on a southbound goods train or freight vessel. I would follow the road for a bit until hopefully I struck a fork leading eastwards. If I found none I would just have to take to the heather again, a prospect I found most unattractive.

Though the valley seemed to be trending north of east, I decided to take advantage of being on a good walking surface for as long as possible.

A bridge crossed the river which issued from the loch, then I was forced to make a detour round a cluster of lit-up huts — a converted Mountain Rescue post, I later discovered. When I next struck the road it had a tarred surface. Headlights appeared in front and I crouched in the heather till the vehicle, a military Land Rover, tore past. A few minutes later the same thing happened from the other direction. Twenty minutes after that an army truck and a motor-cycle approached each other, both pulling up as they came level with the spot where I had taken cover. My ears picked up fragments of conversation above the idling engines.

".. cordons... Balmoral tae Aboyne... and Glen Esk in the south... Strachan tae Fettercairn... pickets... sealed aff the end o' the loch by noo..."

The vehicles roared away. Screening the light from my torch with a handkerchief, I examined the maps. Balmoral to Aboyne represented a stretch of Deeside, running west to east. Glen Esk formed a roughly parallel line to the south. Strachan to Fettercairn made a line to the east, running north and south to connect the other two lines. These key points would be the knots in the strong outer cable of the dragnet set to catch me. Tonight, when only the roads could be closely watched, I must press on as far and as fast as I could towards the eastern perimeter of the encircling cordon. With the sun's next rising, the dragnet would begin to tighten and, unless I could find a gap to slip through, it could catch me in its meshes.

In an extraordinary way the realisation of all this acted as a kind of tonic and my mood of despair began to lift. Faced with a straightforward challenge, I felt I could rise to the occasion. It was only when I thought again of Rachel that anxiety threatened to paralyse my nerve processes.

The night had turned clear with a slice of moon in a star-powdered sky. As long as I could see The Plough I could get a fix on the Pole Star and check my direction. I left the road and struck up a glen to my right. After a long, steady pull I reached the summit of a ridge and picked up an east-flowing stream.

I have no clear memory of the events of that night, just a kaleidoscopic impression of toiling up and down glens furred with dense, shaggy heather and over summit plateaux seamed by peat hags.

At last the sky lightened ahead of me. A light drizzle began to patter on my clothing as dawn broke. I dropped down a hillside to the head of a long and noble glen winding away to the east. This was the valley of the

Water of Aven — not to be confused with my old friend the Avon of the Cairngorms.

By the early forenoon of a warm, showery day, the glen's canyon-like walls began to dwindle and draw back till I was walking on level, marshy haughs. Then, round a bluff in a bend of the river, the ground fell away below me in a vast undulating sweep of heathery moorland rolling away to a dark line of fir plantations. Beyond the forestry stretched a green and yellow checkerboard of fields dotted with the white cubes of farm buildings — the lowlands of the eastern seaboard!

Then I saw something else: between myself and the forestry crawled a long, long line of tiny dots. It was the outer edge of the dragnet. As I watched the approaching cordon, I knew that my moonlight marathon had all been for nothing. Only grouse or hares could have found cover on that open expanse. The dots looked too closely spaced to allow me to slip through unobserved. If I doubled back I would find myself boxed up in the glen, for I lacked the strength to gain the tops behind me or keep ahead of the cordon for very long.

I sank down in the heather in a kind of stupor. The rain was increasing. A numbness seemed to seize hold of my mind so that I watched the creeping line with something approaching apathy. It was almost a relief to be forced to give up, to cease from struggling and just let events take their course.

The cordon approached slowly but remorselessly and was now only a few hundred yards off — a line of poncho-clad figures with slung sub-machine guns. Idly I reflected that my appearance lacked only a Balmoral bonnet to be identical to theirs. The implication bored its way through to where my mind was still functioning at a rational level. I suddenly realised that the game was not yet up, that I still had one card left to play: the old adage which advised 'If you can't lick 'em, join 'em'. One moment I was slack as an un-nocked bowstring, the next I was taut and alert as adrenalin fired the bloodstream.

I pulled up the hood of my poncho to hide my black face as much as possible. I about-turned and as I caught sight of the first figure in the corner of my eye, rose to a crouch and began to walk forward, straightening up as I did so.

My heart pounded wildly as I counted twenty steps... thirty... forty... my ruse was paying off!

Then I froze in sick despair as a voice somewhere on my right bellowed out, "Hey you!

"Aye you, Lofty, wi' yer hood up. Ye're ower far forrit. Git back intae line."

Limp with relief, I waved acknowledgement and dropped back till I was level with dimly-seen figures twenty yards on either side of me. The glen began to close in. Thanks to my station in the line I found myself walking along the lip of the southern wall. The figure to my left vanished behind a hummock. I crouched down and the valley floor to my right disappeared out of my field of vision. A line of heads bobbed briefly against the skyline in front of me then vanished. I counted slowly to five hundred then cautiously raised my head. Not a soul in sight. I was through the dragnet!

14

Lone Star II

I WAITED ten more minutes. Then, crouching low, I doubled back down the glen the way I'd come, not straightening up till I reached the flat expanse of the moor. How far to the coast? I had no exact idea of the distance, but I thought it could not be much above twenty miles.

I hurried across the moor, feeling exposed on its open surface, then cast about along the woodshore till I found a track. This led me through the forestry to a field where on the other side of a drystone dyke, I could hear the putter of farm machinery and the faint burr of broad lowland voices. Propped against the wall was a bicycle. Here was a God-given opportunity. I dumped the gun back in the forestry then, feeling a bit guilty, mounted the machine. Stealing revolvers or machine guns from the enemy was fair game, but it somehow went against the grain to pinch a farmhand's only means of transport.

Reckoning that I would be well advised to keep clear of Deeside with its busy main roads, I detoured south and east along minor roads, heading for Stonehaven. I made good time on the bike and began to feel almost cheerful. Then, early in the afternoon, when I was within a mile or so of the town, a shooting brake slowed down beside me. The driver, a sharp-eyed young fellow, gave me a searching glance, appeared to say something to his girl friend in the passenger seat, then accelerated off down the road.

This could mean only one thing — my captives in the shooting lodge had been set free and my present description circulated; earlier, of course, the dragnet had been trying to catch a yellow-haired Caucasian in an anorak, not a ponchoed negro. If that couple in the Vauxhall were off to report to the nearest authorities, I would be taken in no time unless I found cover. I glanced round despairingly at the bare harvested fields and foursquare farm buildings. No cover there.

I dismounted where a sandy lay-by on the right of the road made a bight in a strip of coniferous wood adjoining the road at rightangles. The lay-by was bordered with stacks of sawn lumber and heaps of trimmed branches beneath one of which I concealed the bike and poncho. Then I followed a track along the inside of the strip which presently joined up with an extensive patch of forestry. Here the track ended.

Struggling through the whippy branches and briars between the close-packed boles was a trying business, but more serious was a continuous clatter of rising wood-pigeons disturbed by my progress, which I was afraid might perhaps alert some watchful keeper or forestry worker. Heading in what I hoped was the direction of the sea and keeping within the forestry, I waded across a small river and crossed a railway cutting — its steep banks matted with vicious gorse — and a forestry road. With scratched face and torn clothing, I emerged at last from the wood where it debouched onto a road. Beyond the road stretched open farmland — plough and pasture, dotted with substantial farm buildings.

I crossed this dangerous stretch, zigzagging at a crouch behind hedges and stone dykes, and eventually gained the cover of another wood. Thus, moving from one woody stepping-stone to another, I traversed fields and roads to reach the coast unseen. Keeping my direction proved no problem as I could see on the skyline an arresting circular structure like a Greek temple — for a moment I thought I was starting to hallucinate. Then I realised it was a war memorial set high above the cliffs of Stonehaven.

From the memorial I looked out over a dramatic, cliff-girt coastline all seamed with bays, rocks and promontories. Southwards a ruined castle reared from the edge of the cliffs. To the north, fringing a crescent of wide sandy beach enclosed by a huge horseshoe-shaped bay, was Stonehaven. Beyond a central gridiron of solid, grey, Georgian and Victorian buildings sprawled an industrial estate, a vast caravan park, its rows of distant vehicles resembling tiny white bricks, and camping-sites packed with multi-coloured tents interspersed with orange-roofed buildings. Westwards a panorama of undulating farmland and forestry rolled back from the coast towards distant blue hills.

In a minute or two I had reached the bluffs containing the southern edge of the bay and looked down onto a harbour in which were moored several familiar vessels. Clearly the oil boom had struck Stonehaven. Like aircraft-carriers amid junks, vast surrealist structures of steel and concrete — the industry's new shore installations — towered above the huddle of ancient crow-stepped buildings and twisting lanes that fringed the harbour.

Selecting a point where the gradient was less steep, I scrambled down the cliffs to the harbour, only to find its approaches sealed off by a raw, new chain-link fence, too high to climb. Beyond the fence I could see a complex of brash new warehouses and offices, with cranes and the upper works of ships showing above them. Everywhere were crates, containers, oil drums, trucks, fork-lifts, storage tanks. Making sure no-one was about, I approached the gate. From a lane between two ancient, dilapidated warehouses I watched the entrance. Ten minutes passed during which time two cars and several seamen passed through without being checked. When the coast was clear, I left my shelter, stepped through the gate and moved behind a stack of tarpaulin-covered stores.

What late-afternoon activity I could observe from my vantage point seemed leisurely and in a low key — cranes swinging cargo, officials checking items on clip-boards, fork-lifts delivering loads. Yet the unhurried tempo was deceptive, I suspected, and really underscored efficiency and economy of effort. That was all to the good from my point of view. If everyone were concentrating on their jobs, they would be less likely to notice a lone individual, conspicuous by his anorak, sheath knife and black skin. Perhaps after all not so conspicuous, I thought, as two negro seamen strolled past. I'd heard that Honduran negroes were fairly common among the crews of supply boats for the oil rigs. If only I could manage to patch up my disguise, I might survive the odd chance encounter long enough to be able to stow away on a south-bound vessel. I would have to try to find something to conceal my top half — seamen don't wear hiking anoraks — and while some of them may carry knives, they don't sport them belted round their waists. I could have got rid of the Bowie, I suppose, but it would go against the grain to have abandoned such a trusty ally.

I took stock of my surroundings. Facing me, about forty yards away on the other side of a complex of light railway lines, was a dingy concrete building, bearing above its door the legend Seamen's Recreation Centre. That might have possibilities. When I was sure that no-one was about, I walked purposefully but unhurriedly across the rails.

I entered the building. To my right an open doorway gave me a glimpse of sailors sitting at tables, drinking from mugs or playing at cards. A smell of frying wafted to my nose. I hadn't thought about food for many hours but now I realised how long it was since I had eaten and I began to feel ravenously hungry. None of the sailors glanced at me. In front of me, at the end of a corridor, was a door with the blessed word 'toilet' on it. And hanging from pegs in the corridor was an array of seamen's caps, donkey-jackets, pea-jackets, storm-jackets and duffel-coats. Ten minutes later, shaved — my Bowie hadn't lost its edge — and with my tinted contact lenses reinserted, I re-emerged to select a navy-blue donkey jacket and a battered seaman's cap. The jacket reached halfway to my knees concealing anorak and Bowie, and the cap sat snugly on my woolly curls. It was hard luck on the owners, but needs must when the devil drives.

I left the building and headed for the harbour. In one of the two basins several chunky little boats rode at anchor, dwarfed beneath their towering radar masts. These I guessed would be tugs, used for towing rigs to drilling sites. In the other basin were berthed several extra-ordinary-looking craft that suggested the offspring of a barge mated with a destroyer. The fore part of each ship swept up in a series of steps to a high, sharply-angled bow with squat funnel, cabin block and bridge rising above the hull. Aft, the vessel fell away to nothing — a mere shallow platform resembling an overgrown tea tray, piled with crates, drums, and various bulky objects under tarpaulins. A curious bridge-like structure — a sort of square archway — spanned the vessel where the fore and aft parts met. These were clearly supply boats, loaded with stores and spare parts for the oil rigs.

"Yo lookin' foh somethin', boy?"

I turned, to see a beefy, overalled figure standing beside me.

My mind raced. "I have a friend on one of these boats," I said glibly, in what I hoped was a Spanish inflexion. "I do not remember which one, except that she is heading south. I want to give a message before she sails."

"*Lone Star II* — she'll be the one yo lookin' foh." He jerked his chin at a supply boat berthed on the far side of the dock. "Bound foh Gannet Field, then Leith. Castin' off in 'bout an hour. Move yo ass, boy, and don't tarry when yo sees yo friend. Cap'n Nicoll don't like no nigras hangin roun' his ship."

That man will never know how close he came to landing on the dock with a broken jaw. I hope that one day some 'nigra' stands up to him and gives him what he deserves. But I couldn't afford to indulge in such luxuries just then, so I thanked him and headed for *Lone Star II*, my fury over the man's arrogance mingled with relief at having found a southbound vessel. My disguise had passed the test with flying colours. If it had taken in a redneck from the Deep South, it would fool anyone.

I strolled unobtrusively along the wharf beside *Lone Star II*. Loading appeared to have been completed. Some deckhands were working on the fore part of the ship, which had a Saltire fluttering at the stern, and a man was tinkering with the radar mast. I scanned the array of cargo aft. The oil drums and crates offered little cover but near the stern, on the port side, was lashed a huge, orange-painted steel cylinder, closed at either end by a massive steel cap and with various oddly-shaped projections sticking out.

Two seamen were securing the lashings on another tarpaulin-covered container. After five minutes they knocked off, climbed a companion-way leading to the fore part of the vessel and disappeared through a cabin door. I stepped onto a truck's tyre-fender between the boat's side and the wharf, balanced on the gunwale and dropped to the deck. As I had hoped, the triangular-sectioned tunnel between the curving side of the cylinder and the right-angled junction of deck and gunwale, was large enough for me to crawl into. I grabbed a coil of thick nylon rope from between two crates and crawled with it into my lair.

I bunched up a wad of rope and stuffed it into the head end of my tunnel, then manipulated more rope with my feet until I had sealed off the outer end. I reckoned that unless someone deliverately came prying into my hiding place, I was secure from discovery. A great wave of weariness seemed to roll over me, now that the need for action and alertness had been temporarily removed. Despite the total lack of comfort in my situation, I was so slogged-out that I dropped within seconds into a profound sleep.

15

The Steel Kraken

I AWOKE cold and cramped, with a dull headache and feeling little refreshed. I must have slept for several hours as no light issued through chinks in my hiding-place. Below me the deck was pitching slightly. I pushed aside the mass of rope blocking the head end of my tunnel and looked out. It was a clear, starlit night with a stiff breeze blowing. There seemed to be no-one on the cargo deck. I reckoned I could risk leaving my tunnel for a few minutes, to flex some of the stiffness from my joints and get some fresh air. I crept out and straightened up painfully in the lee of a tarpaulin-covered mound of cargo.

I peeped over the top of the tarpaulin and gaped at the sight that met my eyes. About a quarter of a mile ahead, silhouetted against the sky, a fantastic object towered above the sea — a wedding-cake in Meccano magnified a billion times. Supported on eight steel pillars was an enormous multi-decked structure the length of two football pitches that suggested a cross between a factory and the upper works of a ship. There were box-like steel buildings, pipes, catwalks, girders, and on either side — like monstrous fishing-rods projecting over the water, hooks swinging from the ends of cables — two gigantic cranes. Rearing up hundreds of feet above the platform was a latticework version of Cleopatra's Needle — the derrick.

The rig blazed with lights — swinging arc-lights, fixed lights that picked out its outline, and high up at the top of the derrick, a solitary red light. A strange medley of sea-muted sounds came to me across the water from the rig, clangs, clanks, metallic squeals and rumblings — the breathing of a steel Kraken risen from the ocean. Here in the North Sea, I sensed, pulsed the lifeblood of Tam Linn's Scotland — black blood, pumped through steel arteries along the sea bed, bringing strength and vigour to the rebel nation. At Cromdale Westminster had lost time, face

116

and the tactical initiative. Here was where they should have struck — at Scotland's soft underbelly and the source of her power.

But it was no time to stare and dream. The supply boat was closing fast with the rig. I relieved myself over the side and crawled once more inside my lair. Shortly afterwards, a hum of activity broke out on the supply boat. Voices called, feet thumped down catwalks to the cargo deck. The boat slowed, shuddered and came alongside the rig with a bumping of fenders. Light shone through the crack between my steel cylinder and the gunwale. A clatter and whine of machinery started up as one of the cranes, I supposed, began to unload stores from the supply boat. Suddenly I went hot and cold as a thought struck me. What if the cylinder under which I was hiding was part of the cargo for this rig? I waited in an agony of helpless apprehension while the unloading went on. At last, to my enormous relief, the noise of the crane stopped. Soon after, the supply boat's engines started up and the deck began to pitch beneath me as the vessel pulled away from the rig.

My sleep must have done me more good than I had realised, for I found that I could think fairly clearly and constructively once more. I must be ready to jump ship the moment she touched the wharf at Leith. In the bustle of tying up, with drilling crew members from the platform going ashore on leave, there was a good chance that I wouldn't attract particular notice. Before any of the deck hands came onto the cargo deck, I would move to the fore part of the boat and try to blend into the landscape. Then, when she berthed, I would join the crowd of offshore men as they streamed onto the wharf. Once ashore, I would lie low until nightfall in a derelict warehouse or a car dump or something similar. Then, travelling by night and hiding up during the day, I would make for Berwick, which I thought was probably the nearest point on the Border. How far was Berwick from Leith? Not above fifty or sixty miles, I thought. I could be there in under forty-eight hours of berthing, if my muscles didn't let me down.

But things didn't work out like that.

Mercifully (for I am a poor sailor), the sea was fairly calm with only a slight swell running, but enough to make *Lone Star II* pitch and roll a bit. I must have slept intermittently for several hours after leaving the rig. I came awake and looked up at a strip of paling sky showing between cylinder and gunwale. Inconsequentially, I observed that the crack seemed to be expanding and contracting, then drifted into sleep again. I must have sunk into a state of profound unconsciousness this time.

I dreamt that Docherty was trying to kill me. We were in McKendrick's, facing each other across a cleared space in the middle of the floor. Docherty was armed with an entrenching tool and I had a tin mug to defend myself with. A silent crowd, all dressed in Hodden Grey were ranged round the walls. Uncle Shamus stood between Docherty and myself, holding a handkerchief which turned into a revolver and crashed onto the floor. Docherty brought down his weapon in slow motion and I fended if off with the mug. Clang! He swung again and once more I parried. *CLANG!*

I jerked awake, opening my eyes. Above me, a thread of sky expanded suddenly into a broad ribbon, then dwindled again. The cylinder, leaping in the wooden chocks that were wedged between it and the deck, fetched up against the gunwale with a deafening reverberation. Muzzily, my brain grasped the fact that the motion of the boat must have caused the cylinder to begin working loose from its lashings. I suddenly realised that I was in a horribly dangerous position below this rolling steel juggernaut, also that deckhands could be expected to arrive at any second to secure the rogue cargo. I scrambled out of my hiding-place and glanced round.

Most of the deck cargo had gone. The sun was well up. Four or five miles to port was a green smudge of coastline. Closer to, on the port side a cliff-girt island thrust up out of the sea. I heard boots thump on steel; two deckhands were climbing down the companionway leading from the fore part of the boat to the cargo deck. There was no real choice. If I stayed, I would be held for questioning and my cover probably blown. If I swam for it, I reckoned I could reach the island, less than a quarter of a mile away if not the shore.

If I still wasn't fully awake as I slipped over the side, I most certainly was a moment later when the cold shock of the sea closed over my head. I stayed under for as long as I could. When I broke surface, I was surprised to see how far away the supply boat was. Treading water, I struggled out of my donkey jacket and anorak and began to swim towards the island. I glanced again at the supply boat, but she continued steadily on her course.

Several minutes later, with fear and cold beginning to clutch at my heart, I realised that I was further from the island despite swimming strongly. There must have been some current in the area against which, in my weakened state, I was unable to make headway. Slowly, the island began to sink back into the sea.

Then my ears picked up a sound — a boat's engines, faint at first but rapidly increasing in volume. As my head lifted on a wave, I saw a white blob heading towards me from the direction of the island. The blob grew, took on definition, then became a gleaming white yacht. She accelerated till she was fairly streaking through the water. The hum of the engines changed to a deep booming; then the craft lifted out of the sea and skimmed along above the waves like an enormous flying fish.

The hydrofoil swirled round me in a tight, foaming circle, then slowly lowered herself into the water as she pulled up, only yards away. I was surprised at how small she looked in the water. A man, dressed in black overalls, appeared on the deck and extended a boathook towards me. I grabbed it and was pulled in like a gaffed salmon. He helped me up a ladder on the side then without a word showed me into a cabin. The yacht began to move. As the rumble of the engines changed to a deep booming, the bows lifted and she hurtled back towards the island.

My memories about what happened immediately after being picked up are dim. I vaguely remember the hydrofoil berthing in a cave opening to the sea at the foot of the cliffs, then being marched, dripping, up a steep flight of stairs hewn out of the living rock of the island. We surfaced in a courtyard surrounded by ancient stone buildings straight out of a horror film. A small reception committee of young toughs in black track suits then escorted me down stone corridors into a cell-like room. A white-coated figure plunged a syringe into my arm. My last dreamy thoughts before drifting into unconsciousness were that I might have found sanctuary in some Outward Bound School or a scientific research station of some kind. If that were so, it was conceivable that I had fallen into the hands of neutrals or even potential friends.

I opened my eyes, feeling clear-headed and refreshed. I was in bed in a small, white-painted chamber. Through a pointed window I could see clouds tinged with pink from the setting sun. The only other furniture apart from the bed was a chair on which a young, alert-looking man was seated. He had that indefinable air of toughness and competence which you sense in professional sportsmen or athletes. He had close-cropped red hair and wore a black track suit. Seeing me awake, he pressed a bell in the wall.

"Where am I?" As an original opener it didn't score many marks but it seemed appropriate in these unexpected surroundings.

The young man glanced at me with cold eyes. "Get up," he said, ignoring my question.

This didn't sound too encouraging, but I willingly complied. I saw that I was dressed only in underpants, startlingly white against the blackness of my skin.

The door opened and another young man, also with an old-fashioned military haircut and dressed in black track suit, came in.

"Clothes?" I suggested, still feeling quite at ease, perhaps as some residual effect of the drug I had been given.

This too was ignored. I found myself fallen in between the two young men, being marched down a stone corridor then up a spiral staircase and halted in front of a massive wooden door. One of my escorts pressed a bell. A green light came on above the door and we entered a huge room whose vaulted stone roof was supported on massive pillars. Golden evening light poured through Gothic windows.

At the far end of the room a man sat writing at a kneehole desk with his back to me. Although the face was invisible, there was something disquietingly familiar about the figure. A longish pause ensued during which the only sound was the faint scratching of pen on paper. A chill descended on my good spirits. Then the seated man carefully blotted the page, screwed up the fountain pen and slowly turned round to face me.

My stomach churned with sick despair. My mind did a double-take, as the scene in McKendrick's bar flashed before my eyes. For the face beaming at me, with a smile of welcome contorting its death's head features, belonged to the man whom in all Scotland I was least anxious to meet again.

16

The Eagle's Nest

"WELL, WELL — this *is* a pleasant surprise," purred Maclean, in his softest lilt. "Jimmy — Mr Wainwright'll be wanting food and a bath and a change o' clothes. Chust see to it now. No hurry, Mr Wainwright," Skull-face went on in soothing tones. "No hurry at all, at all. You'll feel more yourself when you've had a bite and a nice hot bath. Then we can have a wee chat over a dram, eh?"

I'd read about the method, I reflected gloomily as I leaned back in a steaming bath some time later, feeling the stiffness melt away from my muscles. It was standard practice behind the Iron Curtain. You first bullied the prisoner, then after an interval gave him VIP treatment. Then back to the shouting and slapping routine for a time. It was supposed to be very effective in breaking a prisoner's morale and resistance. I could well believe it.

I dried myself then looked into the mirror. My disguise had taken some dents. A bald negro, with one blue and one grey eye, stared back at me, the sea having removed wig and contact lenses. A fuzz of yellow stubble showed through the black skin on jaws and scalp. This I removed with a razor, more for the sake of comfort than to patch up my disguise whose raison d'etre must surely now be finished for good.

Physically I didn't feel too bad, although still rather weak and stiff. Morale-wise I had about as much fighting spirit as a tame white rabbit, although the Wainwright brand of fatalism provided, I suppose, a kind of substitute.

Putting on the track suit and baseball boots which were provided, I pressed an electric bell. The same two guards escorted me back to the great chamber, now lit by strip-lighting along the panelled walls. Maclean was seated in an easy chair by the fireplace, in which an electric imitation coal-fire flickered.

"Come and sit ye down, Mr Wainwright," Skull-face said solicitously, waving me into an easy chair on the other side of the fire. "Ye'll take a drop o' Lion's Milk?" he went on, pouring a golden liquid from a flask into two liqueur glasses. "Distilled from a secret formula invented by the monks of Inchcraig and since handed down from tenant to tenant of the island. Sleanthe!"

I was going to need all the courage I could get, Dutch or otherwise, so I accepted his proffered glass. The stuff was good — sweet and fiery with a taste something between Glayva and Drambuie. While we sipped, Maclean nattered away smoothly about the history of Inchcraig. Set in the mouth of the Forth, midway between the Isle of May and the Bass Rock, Inchcraig had first been settled by monks in the reign of David I. Most of the present buildings dated from the mid-twelfth century and the following three centuries.

After the Reformation the island had passed into the hands of various families. It had been held successively by Patrick, third Earl of Ruthven, leader of Rizzio's murderers, briefly by Regent Morton before his downfall and execution by a prototype guillotine, then by the Erskines, and after a brief period as a garrison for Cromwellian troops by the Nisbets, in whose hands it had remained until purchased by the National Trust for Scotland. This body had bought the island partly because of its historic buildings and partly on account of its unique colony of seabirds — shearwaters, fulmars, puffins, gannets.

After UDI Inchcraig had been commandeered by the Scottish Republican Army as a combined Intelligence HQ, munitions depot and training centre for an elite corps of special agents, the Eagles, hence the island's nickname — the Eagle's Nest. Inchcraig's isolation, splendid community buildings, underground chambers and rugged terrain made it ideal for all these purposes. Maclean was commanding officer with a staff mainly composed of instructors, technicians and quartermaster-sergeants in charge of the various departments.

An intake of fifty young Eagles was at present undergoing training on the island. It was one of these, on look-out duty, who had spotted me in the sea. The hydrofoil provided a fast ferry service for top-brass visiting the Eagle's Nest from Edinburgh. On calm days the hydrofoil could cover the distance between Leith and Inchcraig — twenty-five miles — in half an hour flat.

"We are forging here the spearhead of the Scottish nation," Maclean murmured, and his deep-sunk eyes in the death's-head face gleamed with a fanatical light. "Not a shield, Wainwright, but a spear — a spear of tempered steel. It is not enough for Scotland passively to resist her foes. To be secure and strong, she must seek out and destroy her enemies wherever they exist. For it is Scotland's destiny one day to rally the ancient peoples of the West — Scots, Welsh, Irish, French, Iberians and our kinsfolk across the Atlantic in Nova Scotia and French Canada, and among the Irish in North America — the scattered fragments of the once mighty Celtic race that held sway across Europe from Spain to Russia. A truly great people whose achievements are not to be measured by barren conquests and stupid piles of stone but in things of the spirit — in the beauty of a curving line, in poetry, in song."

Maclean picked up a small object from the desk beside him and thrust it before my face. It was a small gold brooch most exquisitely chased with a linear design, the lines weaving and interlocking in a complex and beautiful pattern.

"That, Wainwright, came from the grave of a Gallic chieftain who lived perhaps a hundred years before Julius Caesar. But it might equally have come from Ireland or the Crimea. It is the apotheosis of the Celtic spirit, the spirit of freedom, of the high and open places. What happened to these people, Wainwright? They were destroyed — crushed between the nether millstone of the conquering Roman legions and the upper millstone of the German savages driving down from the Baltic. We fought back of course: you have only to think of Vercingetorix, of Caradoc, of Boudicca, of Arthur. Did you know that in the tenth century Scots, Irish, Welsh and Bretons formed a Celtic League to resist the Norsemen? But always our foes were too strong, too organised — disunity was ever our Achilles heel. In Britain there triumphed 'Mi-run mor nan Gall' — the great hatred of the Gael, which the Saxon has always felt towards the Celt. A policy of genocide, as deliberate as the extermination of the Red Indian in America, began in the Middle Ages with Letters of Fire and Sword issued against clansmen by the Privy Council and reached its full flowering in the Massacre of Glencoe, in the aftermath of the '15 and the '45 and in the Clearances. Where once a free and noble people lived, now only the stag and the Cheviot roam. Culloden was the last flicker of Celtic resistance. Until August of this year.

"What has replaced the living culture of the Celts, Wainwright?" Maclean's voice had lost all its urbanity and vibrated with passionate conviction. His eyes now had a fixed, glazed look as though he were looking at something far off, something invisible to myself. "The dead cultures of the Teutonic North and the Roman South, of the forest and the forum, with their legacy of materialism and greed, of bloodthirsty repression, of soul-shrivelling laws and deadening mores — these have replaced the Celtic heritage. And they have become the inheritance of America, of Japan, of the European Community. They will eventually corrupt all humanity if allowed to spread unchecked. But the ancient Celtic peoples, under the lead of Scotland, will learn to unite at last. When that happens, they will join with their kinsmen of the East to destroy for ever the evil legacy of Germany and Rome."

I listened, fascinated and appalled, to these poisonous half-truths with their sinister echoes of Nazi Germany, of *Lebensraum* and *Herrenvolk* and recalled Rachel's warning about Maclean's Pan-Celtic League. I assumed that the phrase "join with their kinsmen of the East" implied some future pact with Russia — an East-West Axis? Perhaps even a Final Solution of the Latin and Teutonic peoples was envisaged? It was not too difficult to imagine Maclean sending out his Eagles to infiltrate and dominate, by propaganda and political murder, those communities scheduled for Liberation.

"Forgive me, I got a little carried away, I'm afraid." Maclean was once more the affable and courteous host. "Finish your dram and I'll show you around the buildings. This — " he waved a hand around the chamber, "used to be the Abbot's Lodging."

Accompanied at a discreet distance by the two Eagles, I began a conducted tour of the monastery with Maclean acting as guide. I knew of course that he was playing with me, that the charade of hospitality was merely to gratify some quirk of vanity or sadism. Sooner or later the gloves would come off. I dismissed for the time being the idea of trying to make a break. The two Eagles each had the unmistakable stamp of the trained man of action — a sort of relaxed alertness. I knew with total certainty that if I made a dash for it I would be doubled up in agony before I had covered five yards.

Down a spiral staircase into a colonnaded, spotlit courtyard in which groups of Eagles in the ubiquitous black track suits were practising unarmed combat.

"The Cloisters," murmured Maclean. "And now we'll take a look at the Church."

We entered a huge Gothic pile, now fitted out as a lecture theatre with blackboards, projectors and other equipment. Next, I was shown into an

octagonal building in which, apart from a couple of spotlights, the only
light issued from a vast illuminated sheet of frosted glass set in the floor
and surrounded by concentric tiers of benches. A few spectators were
scattered about.

"The Chapter House," Maclean whispered. "We'll sit down and
watch for a wee bit."

The place had been converted into an Operations Room. The great
glass table portrayed on its surface an enormous map of Scotland.
Coloured squares, oblongs and circles, obviously symbolising military
bases, units, and other points, gave a clear picture of the tactical position.
Those red squares must represent forts: I picked out Tomintoul, Derry
Lodge and Balmoral.

"Alpha Zulu to 841278," announced a disembodied voice from beyond
the head of the Table. A spectral hand appeared over the edge of the
Table and with a wooden rake pushed a coloured symbol a few inches
along the National Boundary line. A Border Patrol perhaps? Another set
of co-ordinates was announced and a model black ship was propelled
about a foot along the Lothian coast.

"English Patrol Boat on reconnaissance," whispered Maclean. "It's
from a section of the English Expeditionary Force fleet stationed off
Berwick. And now, if you've seen enough, we'll pay a final visit to the
vaults."

We left the Chapter House and proceeded to an arched doorway in a
corridor leading off the cloisters. This entry was guarded by two soldiers
bristling with grenades and automatic rifles. At Maclean's command one
of the guards unlocked the door, pushed it open and reaching inside
switched on a light. A staircase, hewn out of the island's bedrock,
spiralled downwards. A faint smell of brine came up from whatever lay
below.

"After you," murmured Maclean, ushering me through the door. The
armed guards accompanied us, replacing the previous escort.

The staircase eventually opened into a huge chamber lined with piles
of crates bearing stencilled letters, some of them Cyrillic characters. The
air was cold and stale.

We filed through a succession of cellars, most of which seemed to be
natural caverns, though the connecting passages bore the marks of picks
— "distillery... monks' charnel house... beer cellar... ," Maclean
specified. Whatever their original purpose, each cellar was now piled
high with crates which, Maclean explained, contained weapons and

explosives. The extent of this underground arsenal was staggering —
there seemed to be enough stuff to equip an army. Clearly, stockpiling
had begun long before UDI. The Scottish National Trust must have been
infiltrated by Fiery Cross members who had taken over the running of
the island while preserving a respectable front — yet further proof of the
group's ubiquitous power.

We came to an iron gate barring the passage. Maclean unlocked it and
we entered a circular chamber which contained no exit I could see.
Maclean locked the gate from the inside and pocketed the key.

A cold knot of fear began to tighten inside me as I took in the decor.
Grisly instruments of torture bristled from the walls in a collage of
blades, hoops and spikes. Between these exhibits were cases of explosives
and padlocked racks of small arms. In the centre of the stone-flagged
floor was a round hatch cover made of heavy timber. From somewhere I
could faintly hear the slap of water, but could not remember seeing a
window since leaving the cloisters.

I had a feeling the party was almost over.

"The Guard Room," announced Maclean in conversational tones.
"This was once Regent Morton's torture chamber, used for extracting
information from political prisoners. We decided to keep it in working
order. After all," he added with a chuckle, "you never know when it
might come in useful. Those are the Pirliekins." He indicated a
contraption resembling a sophisticated bottle-opener but which I
suspected was a thumbscrews. "Or, if that didn't obtain the desired
result, there was always the Boot," and he pointed to a leg-shaped iron
frame. "You hammered in wooden wedges — the bones burst eventually. Very effective, so I'm told. Now this — " he waved a hand towards a
squat little guillotine, and his voice took on a connoisseur's zeal, "is
something we just had to have. The Maiden on permanent loan, you
might say, from the National Museum of Antiquities in Edinburgh.
Morton himself was executed in it, you see."

The hatch cover was pulled up and thrown right back with a thud that
echoed round the cell. The mouth of a vertical well-shaft, about three
feet in diameter, was revealed; the odour of brine suddenly became
stronger.

"The oubliette — a one-way exit for difficult prisoners. And that,
Wainwright, concludes our little tour. I hope you have enjoyed it."

Maclean uttered the last sentence in tones of chilling mockery. It got
to me that I was probably going to die in the very near future, possibly in

126

agony. My palms began to sweat and my mouth dried out with fear. Escape seemed quite impossible — the entrance to the chamber was locked and the only other way out was the hole in the floor which led straight to the sea. Somehow, I didn't think there was much future in that. I tried to fight down a surge of panic, but it was a losing battle.

"Well, Wainwright," Maclean rasped, "you can either make it easy for yourself — or extremely painful. The choice is yours. Just tell me everything you know — your contacts, who you've passed on information to, where the document you stole is. You know, after all the bother you've caused us, I find myself rather hoping that you'll be stubborn. Like the Shetlanders were — at first. The task of making them tractable was not without a certain stimulus."

Maclean's sadism sent anger flooding through me, dissolving the paralysis which had begun to take a hold. My mind seemed to click into gear and begin functioning smoothly and swiftly. I wasn't out of the game yet. Not quite. Taking on Maclean and the guards with my bare hands was out. To achieve anything, I had to launch a surprise attack with a weapon of some kind. My eyes swept the chamber. All the torture gadgets were chained or bolted to the walls. Steel chains, running through the trigger guards, secured the small-arms in their racks. Grenades, like iron pineapples, gleamed in boxes. If only they had been primed I might have been able to grab one and create a stalemate. But of course, for safety reasons, the primers were boxed separately.

And then I realised that such a weapon was within my grasp.

If there had been just my own neck to worry about, I doubt if I could have summoned the nerve for my next action. But I was committed to playing the game out to the end, and the rules said that I had to stay alive for as long as possible, even if it meant — as looked exceedingly likely — that I would be prolonging my life by a very short space indeed.

"Nothing to say, Wainwright?" Maclean sneered. "Perhaps we can help to refresh your memory. The Boot, I think. Rory — tie him up."

My chest tightened and a roaring filled my ears, My hand of its own volition, it seemed, flashed out and plucked a grenade from the man's tunic. Naked terror appeared in three pairs of eyes as I yanked out the pin.

I tossed the grenade behind an ammunition box and flung myself feet first into the oubliette.

17
Lapsang with the General

ANYONE WHO has ever jumped down an oubliette will probably back me up when I say it is not an experience one would willingly make into a habit. I hurtled down into total blackness, and splashed — after what seemed an eternity — into icy water. It came just up to my neck. My feet had made contact with an unyielding surface — if felt like a grille of crossed iron bars. Fortunately the shaft's walls were smooth, otherwise I would probably have suffered severe abrasions.

Upstairs it sounded as if they were having quite a party, to judge by the din. In a distracted sort of way I had been aware of the grenade going off above me as I descended the shaft. Now, a whole series of thuds could be heard up there, presumably boxes of HE exploding. Something yielding and sticky — I didn't like to think what — bounced off my head and there was a splash. A blazing fragment from a wooden crate shot past and vanished with a hiss, but not before its light had given me a momentary glimpse of my surroundings.

A few inches below my chin water gleamed. Assuming it was sea water, as the tide rose the victim — unable to climb the smooth walls of the shaft — would drown when he eventually became too exhausted to swim. In time his skeleton would fall apart, the bones would drop through the grille and sink down the shaft out into the sea. All very neat and simple. And probably foolproof, I realised with a stab of panic.

But I wasn't given any time to mull over my predicament. The shaft rumbled violently and a blast of hot air slammed down onto me as a vast explosion beat at my eardrums. I guessed that flame and splinters, flashing through the torture chamber's gate, must have set off explosives in the adjoining storage cave. Then I found myself being hurled violently to and fro as the enclosing stone leapt and shuddered, a hurricane of searing, fume-laden air roaring around my head. Bang after deafening bang sounded from above. Stone fragments showered down on me. I took a deep breath and ducked under.

Suddenly, the bars below my feet gave way and I plunged down into icy water. I surfaced, gasping for air, and drew in a lungful of fumes and dust. The crumbling of the oubliette's walls must have caused part of the grille to become dislodged. I scrabbled at the stone and a huge lump broke off in my hands. I had just enough presence of mind to retain my hold on it as the water closed over my head once more and I was sliding swiftly downwards.

That descent down the water-filled shaft was, I think, the most hideous experience I have ever undergone. To be shut up in an enclosed space is unpleasant enough, especially if you suffer from mild claustrophobia. Fill that enclosed space with water and extinguish all light and the horror of the situation is scarcely to be borne.

My lungs were on the point of bursting when at last the containing walls of the shaft drew back and a wavering lightness appeared far above my head. I released the stone and began kicking out.

When I broke the surface I was for a time too busy gulping down air to notice what was going on. Then, treading water, I struggled out of the track suit and began to swim as hard as I could away from the trembling cliff face which towered into the blackness above.

Vast, muffled explosions boomed away behind me and I was continually jolted by shock waves. I looked back over my shoulder and saw a fantastic fireworks display. Silhouetted dramatically on top of the great stack of Inchcraig, the monastery buildings spouted flame in a hundred places. The initial explosion must have set off a chain reaction which was causing the whole arsenal to go up. Even as I looked the great church seemed to swell, then suddenly it disintegrated and where it had stood a gigantic column of fire writhed up into the night sky, accompanied by a bang of Krakatoan magnitude.

After that I didn't stop swimming until I had covered several hundred yards, most of it under water to avoid the chunks of rock and masonry that rained down into the sea.

As the reverberations died down, the singing in my ears gave way to another sound — the thresh of a ship's propellers somewhere ahead of me. I raised myself as high as I could out of the water and saw moving lights heading in my direction.

The ship stopped about a hundred yards away, and amidships a dazzling cone of light sprang out and proceeded to sweep the surface of the sea. Desperately, I tried to avoid the searchlight; drowning was almost preferable to recapture. But my muscles were beginning to knot with cramps after being subjected to this treatment twice within twenty-four hours and I was too exhausted to manage to stay submerged for more than seconds at a time. The probing beam scythed towards me. I dived, only to surface in the middle of a blinding circle of light. I tried desperately to swim clear, but the beam tracked me remorselessly. I heard the putter of an outboard engine and a dinghy burst through the circumference of the beam's section. Hands gripped my arms and I was hauled struggling over the gunwale.

"Keep still, Sambo, ferchryssake," growled a voice.

"Let the bleeder drahn," someone else chimed in. "Bloomin' Scotch Spyde. I'd shoot every one of them haggis-eatin' bastards if I had the chance."

"Belay that!" snapped an authoritative voice. "Watch his head on the thwart."

I stopped resisting as I realised that these were English voices. Then I remembered the patrol boat off the Lothian coast that was being tracked in the Operations Room! They must have come along to investigate and to pick up survivors.

"English?" I enquired feebly.

"Yeah — worst luck for you, mate."

I tried to see the captain but was told darkly to "shurrup, Haggis, or yer'll get filled in, see."

We docked at Berwick that night where my request to see someone in authority was again ignored. I was regarded as a bald, black lunatic, and by early morning I was on my way together with five Scots prisoners — all the survivors of the big bang at Inchcraig — to Langley Castle, once a converted girls' school deep in Northumberland, but now a top-security prison.

In retrospect the next few hours seem comic, but at the time I had never felt so frustrated. Desperately aware that time was running out — the deadline, September 11th, was barely ten days away — I demanded an interview with the governor. This was at first refused, but by dint of roaring out 'Onward Christian Soldiers' again and again at the top of my voice, I managed to stir up enough resentment for my request to be eventually granted.

The governor proved to be one of those dreadful autocrats in whom responsibility reinforces strong native streaks of stubbornness, prejudice and integrity. My black face — the skin dye unfortunately was of a long-lasting variety — and somewhat wild manner clearly antagonised him from the start. I realised with bitterness and a sinking heart that he was the sort who would go to the stake rather than show indulgence to what he obviously regarded were the ravings of a dangerous impostor. After a brief encounter culminating in total stalemate — I was shouting and he barely controlling his anger — I was transferred to solitary in one of the corner towers, where any further hymn-singing on my part wouldn't disturb the other inmates of the castle.

Here I fumed in impotent frustration for four days, then on September 5th my luck turned. The governor apparently took to heart his religious responsibilities towards his charges, for on the morning of the fifth a young chaplain was admitted to my cell. He seemed a friendly, sensible sort and I decided to appeal to him. Cutting through his introductory pleasantries, I forced him to listen to my story. Something in my manner seemed to get through to him, for he heard me out in silence with an expression of deepening concern on his boyish, bespectacled face.

"They warned me I'd be dealing with a nutcase," he confided when I'd finished. "But you're clearly as sane as I am and I'd stake my dog collar you're telling the truth. If only you had some proof."

"There's the rub," I groaned. "My only proof's the Russian Agreement and God only knows where that is now."

"Agreement, did you say?" rapped the chaplain, his brows furrowing. "That rings a bell, somehow." He got up hurriedly and called for the guard. "I can't promise anything," he went on mysteriously, "but I'll have a word with the governor. He may just listen this time."

Fifteen minutes later my cell door was unlocked and I was escorted to a driveway outside the castle and bundled into the rear of a security van whose doors were locked behind me. Then the vehicle took off at a fast clip. Through the mesh-covered windows I could see a bleak countryside unrolling — hill pasture criss-crossed by stone dykes, with the occasional grey, weathered farmhouse sheltering in a dip. At one stage the road ran parallel to a massive stone wall switchbacking up and down a great escarpment and topped by a fringe of iron stakes and barbed wire. Swerving, the road plunged through a break in this curious structure and headed straight as an arrow into an expanse of bare moorland.

Soon there appeared signs of large-scale military activity — army vehicles roaring up and down the road, fields converted into gun and vehicle parks or occupied by troops under canvas. Presently, we pulled up in an army camp of wooden buildings. Here I was ushered into the presence of someone I vaguely recognised from photographs and cartoons — that wrinkled forehead, those soulful eyes with deep pouches below them, the drooping moustache and jowls. Just as the introductions were being made, I remembered. It was Lieutenant-General Sir James Basset.

Though I didn't know it at that moment, he had just replaced the Chief of Staff responsible for the fiasco of the British Expeditionary landing on the Moray coast.

The Basset Hound, as the General was inevitably known, was possibly the most unwarlike soldier the British Army has ever produced. Gentle, unflappable, sympathetic and with a certain wry sense of the absurd, Basset preferred diplomatic or economic rather than strong-arm solutions to military problems, and had scored some remarkable successes. For example, when the islanders of a tiny but strategically important West Indian Dependency had rebelled against British rule, Bassett had cooled the situation by staging a cricket match with a free barbecue thrown in for spectators.

After shaking hands and nodding me in the direction of a chair, his only words were "I think we know most of what you're going to say, Wainwright. But let's hear it all the same." The General heard me out in silence. Then, opening the door of his quarters, he stood in the porchway with his hands in his pockets looking out over the moors.

"Pot of tea, Wainwright," he said unexpectedly. "China or Indian?"

A few minutes later, Basset handed me a cup of my old friend Lapsang Soochong. He took a few appreciative sips then announced, "I've good news for you." He went on with a mournful smile, "We've got the Agreement. Thanks to your friend Miss Marenga — a very talented and courageous young woman, if I may say. She persuaded the patrol who so rudely interrupted your — ah slumbers, that you'd forced your way in and demanded food and shelter. What could a helpless woman do when faced with a desperate character like yourself, but comply? When the soldiers called, she tried to detain you, but alas! to no avail. The fact that Miss Marenga is apparently a well-known face to certain people in Scotland helped to convince her military visitors that she was entirely above deceit. She can, I imagine, be very convincing when she sets her mind to it.

"The Caledonians departed eventually, offering commiserations concerning her ordeal at your hands. The following day she arrived by bus in Edinburgh, that villain Wainwright having decamped with her car. Then she entrained for a little town on the Border, which she crossed under cover of night. After contacting the English police, she was eventually passed on to myself. Plus the Agreement. Good show that on your part, Wainwright, by the way. Must see if we can't fix up some sort of gong for you."

"You mean Rachel is safe on this side of the Border?"

Basset poured more Lapsang for both of us in silence, then went on. "When the Agreement was decoded, Westminster took its implications very seriously indeed, and the flap spread to NATO. What you've seen on the way here is only a small part of the force with which we are about to launch a full-scale military invasion of Scotland. By the way, the details of the Agreement and how we got it have been kept from the ears of the vulgar, but the fact that an Agreement exists is fairly widely known — in official circles at least.

Listening to all this, a huge load seemed to slip from me. "It's marvellous news, sir," I said, "about Rachel, and the Agreement — of course. I'd like to see her if that's possible."

Basset looked pensively into his tea cup. "Well, that would be a little difficult, Wainwright. You see, she volunteered to go back over the Border and supply us with information. With her contacts and experience, she managed to get herself taken on as a front-line war correspondent with the Scots. Made a great hit with my equivalent on the other side apparently. Accompanies him all over the place in his Land Rover. Thanks to her, we've got a pretty good idea of their overall strategy; she radioes in every day on a special frequency."

"So Rachel's a spy!" I exclaimed in genuine horror.

"No one knows better than you, old chap, how big the stakes are," Basset said gently. "Nobody else could take on the job she's doing. I don't think you'd really have it otherwise, if you think about it."

He was right — I saw that. But all my elation evaporated, leaving me miserably apprehesive on Rachel's account.

I volunteered for service, of course, and was drafted into Intelligence on Basset's Staff with my old rank of major.

18
Eastern Approaches

ON SEPTEMBER 7TH Basset's invasion force, consisting of mechanised infantry, tanks and artillery with air support, crossed the Border without opposition and on the same day a flotilla from Her Majesty's Fleet steamed into the Forth. Clearly Basset did not intend that Cromdale should be repeated: planning and organisation were smoothly efficient. Meanwhile 'Daft Davie' Campbell concentrated his forces on Edinburgh and rapidly established a chain of defences around the city on the front facing the English advance. Mines were laid in the Forth to deter the English fleet from approaching Leith. To the east of the city sections of the approach roads were blown up, the flat farmland sown with mines and covered with tank traps. A strong defensive line was set up along the River North Esk with the little towns of Musselburgh, Dalkeith, Lasswade and Loanhead forming the key points.

To the south-west of the capital, the Republican forces continued the defensive line along the Pentland Hills — a wild and lonely range rising in places to two thousand feet and extending for close on twenty miles.

The western approaches to the city were only lightly guarded. To attack from that direction the Westminster forces would first have to turn the long, long flank of the Pentlands, giving Daft Davie plenty of time to transfer troops to the other side of Edinburgh.

During the 7th English jets whistled over the environs of Edinburgh, flying back to report to Basset's advancing host. By evening, reconnaissance vehicles were sniffing out the approaches to the city. That night and throughout the next day Basset's forces, approaching via Lauder, proceeded to harbour up opposite the Republican lines on the dead ground behind a low, broken ridge extending from the village of Newtongrange in the north-east to Romanno Bridge in the south-west. Between the two forces stretched a long strip of flat country — in the north the farmlands of the North Esk Valley, in the south a barren expanse of rough pasture and reclaimed bogland known as Auchencorth Moss.

The days passed in a sort of charged calm — beautiful Indian Summer days with the rowan and the beech just beginning to turn gold and copper. Nothing happened apart from an occasional reconnaissance jet screaming across the sky or a scout car from either side scuttling up and down as near to the enemy lines as it dared. Life was quite pleasant. I was enjoying a certain prestige as news of my exploits passed around the Intelligence unit.

The 11th — the day scheduled for Tam Linn's answer to Russia's rocket and submarine base proposals — came and went without, so far as Intelligence could discover, any communication between Edinburgh and the Kremlin taking place. Probably Russia was just waiting to see which way the cat would jump before committing herself.

The hawk faction on Basset's Staff, inflamed by ugly rumours about firing squads and concentration camps in the Shetlands, agitated for immediate tough action, with a massive air strike against the capital as a preliminary. But Basset, perhaps unwilling to create a legacy of bitterness, refused to be stampeded into a premature offensive. Asked by an impatient staff officer what he proposed to do, Basset replied, "Nothing. Mistakes are made only by people who do things," — a typical piece of 'Bassetry' which at once went to swell the store of Basset stories, of which there was a legion.

And so Fabius watched Hannibal.

Daft Davie, with his reputation for panache, was expected to open play. Time was, if anything, against the Scots. The big bang at Inchcraig must have had a serious effect on their reserves of weapons, whereas Basset could draw on virtually inexhaustible supplies and had the Community and NATO behind him. A quick victory was in the Scots' interests.

So it was no surprise when on the 14th a message came from Rachel that large bodies of infantry, armour and artillery were gathering in Dalkeith Park. This was it. Daft Davie was coming out. He was going to deliver a left hook, perform a pincer movement and execute a cutting-out operation. To meet this potential threat, a heavy concentration of English guns and armour was mobilised at Newtongrange opposite Dalkeith.

On the 16th Rachel failed to report on schedule. I was on tenterhooks for the rest of the day, waiting in vain for her callsign to come through. I spent a night of sleepless worry; when she failed to report in, the following day, I managed to get myself an interview with Basset.

Basset waved me onto a seat in his kennel — as his mobile HQ was affectionately known — a kind of self-propelled caravan like an enormous Dormobile.

"Ah, Wainwright — I rather expected you'd ask to see me," he murmured. "I think I know what it is you're going to suggest — a one-man mission into enemy territory to rescue Miss Marenga. Sorry, old chap, but I'm afraid it's not on."

My stomach knotted in desperation. "But surely, sir — "

"Steady on, Wainwright," Basset broke in. "I don't intend to abandon Miss Marenga to the clutches of the Caledonians without making some effort on her behalf. As it happens, one of my best men has had to pull out of a certain operation rather suddenly, and is free at present. I intend sending him back behind the Scottish lines to take Miss Marenga's place and carry on her work. If you wished to accompany him — well, I wouldn't stand in your way."

"Thank you, sir!"

"Yes, well... of course you realise that if anything went wrong you'd be on your own? If you were caught it wouldn't help you much to quote the Geneva Convention."

"Yes, I realise that, sir."

"Also, you'd be under my agent's orders. Supplying key information about the Scots' movements is the main thing, remember. Rescuing Miss Marenga must, I'm afraid, be a side show, only to be attempted if there's no risk to security."

I said that I understood.

"Good. And now I think it's time you met your partner in crime."

An orderly was despatched and, while we waited, Basset ordered tea. We had just taken our first cup when a knock sounded on the Kennel's rear door.

"Enter," called Basset.

My brain whirled and I stared in disbelief as a tall, lantern-jawed individual, with hair sprouting on his high cheekbones, stooped and entered the vehicle.

"Uncle Shamus!" I gasped.

"Colonel Palmer, actually," murmured Basset with a chuckle. "You two have met already, I believe, in somewhat different circumstances. You may divulge, my dear Palmer. Our friend Wainwright is I think perhaps due an explanation."

"Well met, Wainwright," Palmer said, without a trace of Highland accent. He extended his hand with a smile. "As the General says, you deserve to be put in the picture. Couldn't tell you before — top security and all that. Doesn't matter now; my cover for the Rothiemurchus show was beginning to crack and I had to pull out fast."

"You mean — you were running a spy network in the Cairngorms?"

"Well, more of a one-man show, really. I had my regular contacts of course — all trained mountaineers, to give a solid cover. They reported in regularly with political and military information. I couldn't place you at all — it did cross my mind that you might perhaps be a 'plant', sent by Maclean or Campbell to check up on me. Pity we succeeded so well in keeping each other in the dark. I could probably have got you smuggled to the Border via my 'Underground Railway'.

"But — the accent; your age — you looked fifteen years older then; quoting from the Bible... You seemed to know it by heart."

"Well, I do— almost," said Palmer with a rueful smile. "Did a job in Uganda once, smuggling VIP refugees out of the country. Unfortunately, Amin's lads got hold of me and I spent eight months in a Kampala jail. My only reading was a bible that someone had left in my cell. As for the accent and the semblance of age — well, put it down to amateur theatricals. And my appearance was no problem. Although my family have been settled in Norfolk for the past five hundred years, I look like the archetypal teuchter, right down to the fur-bearing cheeks."

Basset produced maps and we settled down to rehearse the details of our mission.

It was a dark night with a powdering of stars when Palmer and I, dressed in the uniform of Republican Army despatch riders, with forged pass-books in the pockets of our Hodden Grey tunics, clambered through the submarine's conning-tower hatch. Away to our left the Lothian coast was a dark smudge, with Dunbar a prickle of lights and the vast bulk of the abandoned nuclear power station at Torness looming blackly against the sky. Some miles to the west, like a deadly necklace hung across the throat of the Firth, under the black water, lay the outer edge of the minefield.

Presently the submarine slowed and rolled gently in the swell. Together with the sailor who was to navigate, we lowered the inflatable rubber dinghy. The sailor pushed off, started the outboard and we puttered off into the darkness.

The dinghy grounded with a soft bump. We scrambled up some low dunes and found ourselves, according to plan, on the edge of a fir plantation. We followed the perimeter round until it turned sharply inland away from the Belhaven Sands. Inside this angle, hidden under piles of brushwood, we found motor-bikes — thanks to a Scottish quisling on Basset's payroll. Our plan was simple and open-ended — to proceed to Dalkeith, mentioned by Rachel in her last report as the scene of large-scale troop movements, then play things by ear. As the Scots had destroyed sections of the main highways, as part of their defensive strategy, we had to thread our way south-westwards along a maze of minor roads.

Outside Dalkeith we were stopped at a roadblock and asked our business by a Republican soldier with sergeant's triple-headed thistle embroidered on his sleeve.

"Despatches for General Campbell," Palmer announced. He seemed totally unconcerned, although my own heart was thumping and my palms beginning to sweat inside their gauntlets. But the man waved us on.

Crossing a river we found ourselves in an area of wooded parkland, brightly-lit by hanging bulbs. The place swarmed like an anthill, with squads of Hodden Grey-clad soldiers being fallen in and marched out. Roped-off sections contained large numbers of tanks, trucks and self-propelled guns. We stood our machines at the side of a great open space, partly filled by massed ranks of Republican soldiers. Clearly something was about to happen, so we stationed ourselves as close as we could to the edge of a roped-off circle in the middle, in which a flagpole bearing the Lion Rampant flag of Independent Scotland rose beside a platform.

An hour passed during which the space gradually filled with troops. Then the whole concourse was brought to attention. A Land Rover raced along a lane in the ranks leading to the central area, skidding to a halt beside the flagpole. A familiar, tall, husky figure in a kilt and Hodden Grey tunic swung himself out of the passenger seat and sprang onto the dais. A spontaneous cheer rippled through the ranks. This was none other than Daft Davie himself, whom I had last seen in conference with Tam Linn at the house near Tomintoul.

Being taller than most of the men around me, I had a fairly clear view of him. Deep-set eyes below mad, flaring eyebrows. Snub nose above a massive chin. The man's stance — feet apart, fists punched onto hips — gave him a look of slightly reckless assurance, an impression strengthened when he began to speak.

He looked slowly round the assembled ranks then blew a raspberry into the mike. "Testing, testing," his voice boomed out above the laughter. "Well, lads," Daft Davie announced, drawing out the words to create a comical yet arresting effect, "now for the Push, as the bishop said to the actress." (Roar) "Sergeant, take that man's name. Ye all ken that General Misfit, or whatever he ca's himself is fleerin' up and down outside o' Newtongrange like an auld wife wi' a dose o' the squitters." (Sniggers) "Silence in the ranks. Well, he's doing just what he's supposed to do — getting ready to meet an attack from the east. Aye, the east. But come the morn's morn, the real attack will come from, wait for it, wait for it — anither direction a'thegither. And how's it to be done, ye're wonderin'? The vital element o' surprise an' a' that. Uncle Davie will tell you. The Met Boys have been working overtime of late and they have predicted — predicted?, they have positively guaranteed — that the fine weather will be followed by fog. The forecast is that by tomorrow morning dense fog will begin to cover the Lothians. We'll ken for sure in a few hours. Assuming that the weather does what it's told, Operation Claymore will begin tomorrow. A huge strike force, drawn from all the camps, will concentrate in a certain place. Where that is, is Uncle Davie's wee secret. Under cover o' the fog, this force will move round behind old Bear's Arse, pinning him up against the Pentland Line. He'll be caught between two fires wi' his thumb in his bum and his mind in neutral. Then we'll have him." (Horse laughs) "Ach, shu' up, you low-minded soldiers. Well, that's all for now. See you at the RV."

And grinning, waving his arms above his head, Daft Davie whirled off amid the solid roar of acclamation.

19
Pentland Rendezvous

AFTER THE TROOPS had returned to their quarters, Palmer and I bivouacked in a summer-house in the park. We spent an hour swapping stories and having a good laugh over the Uncle Shamus episode. Palmer thought that we should stick around and try to discover where the Republican Putsch was scheduled to start from. To break radio silence at this juncture, just to tell Basset that the Scots intended to strike somewhere else than their apparent mustering-point, would be risky and hardly profitable. Better to try to get some hard information before making contact.

I slept but fitfully on one of the wooden benches and we made our toilet in the North Esk at first light. Campbell's Met boffins clearly had done their homework properly, for by the forenoon an early morning haze had thickened into dense fog. Before midday the first vehicles started crawling out of the park. The first stage had begun.

We retrieved our machines and joined the convoy, visible only by the pale blobs of the vehicles' convoy lights wavering through the clammy whiteness. For hours we crawled at a snail's pace along main roads, eventually turning left onto side roads. Time must be getting short. The ground now began to climb and houses were replaced by hedges, trees looming vaguely through the fog-wreaths. I guessed that we were moving into the Pentland foothills. We crossed a bridge over water — a narrow section of Threipmuir Reservoir, I later discovered — and shortly after pulled up in a paddock outside a park wall. The air was filled with the revving of engines in low gear, as invisible vehicles lumbered about in the fog.

We stood our machines by the park wall. Palmer unpacked a radio tranceiver from a saddle-bag, then we proceeded on a tour of exploration. Every few yards a shadowy vehicle would loom out of the mist —

armoured personnel carrier, truck, self-propelled gun. Soldiers huddled in groups beside their vehicles.

We relocated the park wall and followed it along till there was a gateway. We went through the entrance into the park which also seemed filled with troops, guns and vehicles. A distant glimmer of light showing through windows led us towards a large building, the RV headquarters probably. I suggested that our best chance of obtaining information lay there and Palmer concurred.

We had got half-way to the building when I noticed that everything had gone silent. The last vehicles must have got here. A rumour began to ripple through the groups of soldiers. We halted. A fog-muffled tannoy message ordered all personnel to stand by their vehicles. Then a harshly distorted but familiar voice rang out on the tannoy, a voice charged with an emotion and power that still cut through any resistance my will could offer.

"Comrades, this is Tam Linn speaking to you. In a few hours we shall be joined in battle wi' the English. Ye all ken what hangs upon the issue — the survival of Scotland. Make no mistake — if we fail, Scotland will go under for good. Our laws, our education, our customs, our new-found liberty, everything that makes Scotland what she is, and which wi' patience and pride and dogged courage we have striven over the centuries to build up, will be wiped out. Ruthless men of power in Whitehall and Brussels will take over our industries and our new-found wealth from oil, and flood our land wi' alien workers. Our mountains will be raped by foreign mining companies and our glens flooded to create cheap power. The curse of the Clearances and absentee landlord will be repeated on a tenfold scale. Within a generation the Scotland we ken and love will have vanished for ever. But we will not fail. We will never give in. 'For,' in the words of our great Declaration of Arbroath, 'so long as a hundred of us remain alive, we will never in any degree be subject to the dominion of the English, since it is not for glory, riches or honour we fight but for liberty alone, which no good man loses, but with his life.' "

A great swelling cheer burst out as the voice became silent. There was something eerily impressive about the speech, issuing from an invisible source. The cheer rose in volume to a sustained roaring, like breakers on a fog-bound shore, then slowly died away.

Palmer and I set off once more towards the building. Passing a knot of soldiers, I overheard one of them say the words "black lassie".

Immediately, I froze. I conferred with Palmer then slunk unobtrusively up to the group.

"Yon African burd whae used tae be on the telly — her that did the Election Special?" another soldier was asking.

"Aye — that's the yin. Ah heard tell she wiz a spy. Caught wi' a wee radio jist as she wiz aboot tae send aff a message. They've got her in Embro' Castle. She'll be shot. Efter Maclean's Eagles hae finished wi' her, tha' is ."

A roaring filled my ears and something seemed to snap in my brain. I came to myself to find Palmer tugging urgently at my sleeve.

"Come on," he hissed sternly, jerking with his head for me to come away. I followed meekly enough, but despair and horror made me careless. Too late, I reacted to his hand laid urgently on my arm: a sentry with a fixed bayonet materialised out of the fog in front of me.

"Tattie!"

I stood staring stupidly at the soldier, trying to collect my wits. It seemed like some grotesque party game.

"Come on, pal," snapped the sentry, flicking forward the safety catch of his rifle. "Gie us the password."

It was Palmer who saved the situation. He materialised out of the fog suddenly behind the sentry, and tapped him on the temple with the side of his fist. Dropping his rifle, the man slumped to his knees and rolled over on the grass.

"We'll have to get out of the park," whispered Palmer, pocketing a little piece of wood shaped like a darning mushroom. "There's going to be an almighty security flap when they find this." He touched the prostrate sentry with the toe of his boot. "It's essential we get hold of a map with the position of this place marked. Thanks to the fog, I've no idea of our position except that it's somewhere on the northern flanks of the Pentlands."

I was sobering fast, ashamed of the carelessness which had nearly been our undoing. We retreated out of the park, then slipped from vehicle to vehicle, looking into the cabs of those few that were unattended, for a map or any scrap of paper that might tell us where we were or what the destination of The Push would be. I began to feel a growing sense of desperation. Any minute now the huge force might start moving or a hue and cry for ourselves begin. With an enormous effort I forced myself not to think of Rachel — that way madness lay. Our first duty was to warn Basset and for that, above all, a cool head was needed.

Then at last our luck turned. We came across an unoccupied Land Rover with an officer's webbing on the passenger seat — map-case, belt, compass-case. Palmer slid back the window, extracted the compass from its case and pocketed it. Then he took out the map-case and unclipped the cover, revealing a map of the area with chinagraph markings on the talc window.

We oriented the map and began to study it with ferocious concentration. Key positions were marked in with red chinagraphed crosses, routes by dotted lines. The present position of the strike force was at Bavelaw Castle on the north side of the Pentlands, whence a dotted line wound roughly westwards for a mile or two along unmetalled tracks to a farm labelled Listonshiels. From Listonshiels the dotted line continued westwards across country for a further two miles along a footpath to its intersection with another path. This latter path struck almost due south through a great pass between the hills. As far as the head of the pass, the tracks and footpaths had the legend 'Strip Surfacing' chinagraphed over them. Beyond that point the path was labelled 'Old Drove Road'. It eventually debouched onto the A 702 on the south flank of the Pentlands, at the village of West Linton. 'Strip Surfacing' was probably old Second World War perforated steel sheeting used as temporary surfacing for roads or airstrips. The 'Drove Road' must be one of those old cattle trails over which beasts were driven to market before the coming of the railways, and which exist today as broad, turf-clad straps swinging through remote upland country.

The enemy plan seemed clear enough — a push westwards then south through the pass and down the Drove Road to the village of West Linton. Then, in a swift, Panzer-like thrust, the Republican forces would burst from the hills, turn our unsuspecting left flank at Romanno Bridge and race north-east behind Basset's force to link up with their own lines at Dalkeith. The English army, taken by surprise, its communications and intelligence systems hampered by the fog, would be encircled. The circle would contract, and then even I — though hardly an expert in tactics — knew it had been stated as a basic principle of warfare that an army encircled was an army defeated.

Even should the fog eventually clear, this would be to the advantage of the Scots. The chain of Pentland summits — West Kip, South Black Hill, Scald Law, Carnethy, Castlelaw and Caerketton, overlooking the ground onto which the English would be forced to retreat, provided superb sites for observation posts from which a murderous artillery fire could be directed onto the Whitehall forces.

I stared at the fateful pass on the map through which the Scottish spearhead would make the first thrust, a watershed hemmed between two high peaks. The name had a bleak and sinister ring to it — Cauldstaneslap. I was back in Fraser Darling country again, it seemed.

"Breakthrough!" whispered Palmer in a tone of controlled excitement. He tapped the tranceiver. "I'll contact the Basset Hound and put him in the picture. Then... ," he studied the map for a few moments, "I'll get out via this footpath running between Scald Law and Carnethy to the Biggar Road — that's the demarcation line of No Man's Land. Now, off you go and do your Sir Galahad stuff."

"Sure you'll be all right?"

"I'll be fine." Then he added, in his Uncle Shamus voice, "Trust ye in the Lord, for in Jehovah is everlasting strength, Isaiah 25, verse 4."

We shook hands and wished each other luck. Then I hurried back to the park wall and cast about in the fog until I located my machine. Now for Operation Rachel. I pushed the bike onto the road, kicked it into life and moved slowly off downhill, back towards the main road.

20

The Lion's Den

NIGHT WAS falling as I pulled away from the RV. I crawled along uncertainly, my headlamp revealing only an opaque white wall swirling a few yards in front. I re-crossed the causeway over the neck of reservoir, but must have taken a wrong turning after that. Two hours later I had still failed to reach the main road at Balerno.

So dense was the fog that I couldn't even see the junctions of side roads which might lead to farms where I could get directions. I moved in closer to the verge in order to try to spot such openings, and a little later made out a gap in the hedge to my right, distinguishable only as a denser patch of white. I moved gingerly into the opening and felt a rutted surface beneath my wheels. Then, a few yards later, calamity struck. My front wheel began to spin in a muddy patch. I dismounted and started to wheel the machine round the edge of the mire, when the ground to my left suddenly fell away, the bike wrenched out of my hands and vanished. I heard it slithering and crashing away below me; there was a muffled splash followed by silence.

I cursed frenziedly for a minute, just to relieve my feeling of frustration. I groped my way down a steep slope and eventually located the bike lying on its side in shallow muddy water. What I had thought was the opening to a side road must have been the entrance to a field, with the gate pushed back. The 'road' was obviously a cart-track skirting the edge of the field, partly bounded by the bank of a stream.

The next few hours were an agony of impatience and frustration. The thought of what Maclean's animals might be doing to Rachel, while I struggled in mud, fog and water with the motor-bike, threatened to drive me frantic. As last I got it onto the bank and was able to start manhandling it up the slope. This proved desperately slow and exhausting work; I was not yet fully recovered from my wound and was

forced to stop and rest every few minutes. I began to wonder if I should
have come. But eventually I hauled it over the lip of the bank onto the
path. To my enormous relief, we started without trouble and, apart from
a slight wobble of the front wheel, seemed little the worse for wear.

Soon afterwards I reached the main road and turned right, which,
with the Pentlands to my rear, I reckoned ought to be east. Dawn was
breaking — if the term could be applied to a faint luminosity behind the
fog — when a little later I came to a crossroads with signs which gave me
my route for Edinburgh.

The fog was thinner in the city; tall buildings loomed greyly through
shimmering opalescence. At the West End and in Princes Street familiar
landmarks were scarcely recognisable in their sandbag carapaces. In the
Gardens long muzzles of anti-aircraft guns poked from the fog like
knitting needles stuck through cotton wool, reminding me of
Gaberlunzie Night. Now it all seemed totally unreal. The vast, towering
mass of the Castle Rock was a presence felt rather than seen. I rode up the
Mound and turned right up a steep cobbled lane into Castlehill. As I
roared up the Esplanade the stupendous drum of the Half Moon Bastion
loomed above me through writhing coils of vapour.

The guards at the gatehouse, no doubt assuming that my muddy state
betokened urgent news, waved me through after a brief glance at my
pass-book. I bounced up a cobbled way, underneath a great portcullis
gateway with a lion rampant carved above the entrance, then swung up a
curving road ending in a wide irregular space enclosed by shadowy
ramparts and buildings. I dismounted and tried to take stock. Soldiers
with papers and clip-boards, hurrying up and down the entrance stairs of
a great Georgian edifice, made me think this might be Intelligence HQ.
One soldier, a corporal by the double-headed thistle on his sleeve, came
up to me.

"Ony news?" he asked anxiously.

"Sorry. I've just come from Perth," I replied, in what I hoped was a
passable imitation of the correct accent. "What's happening?"

"Ach — it's a bluidy shambles!" he exclaimed. "Bear's Arse must hae
gotten wind o' The Push somehow." I tried to sound shocked. "Seems
he's pu'd his troops richt back. Wurd's jist cam in that he's attackin' Daft
Davie's column frae the flank. Man, if he breaks through we'll be in sair
trouble."

"Aye, we will that," I agreed, stitching a shocked expression onto my
face.

I decided to risk a direct question. "I've to give a message to them that's guarding the black lass," I said. "Her that's being held as a spy."

"Ah heard tell she's in the dungeon aff the Lang Stairs." He pointed to an archway dimly visible in the fog. "Gang through Foog's Gate, then past St. Margaret's Chapel and ye're at the stairheid."

I thanked him and hurried through the archway, past a little rectangular building with Norman windows, and found myself at the top of a steep flight of stairs plunging down between rock face on the left and a massive, crenellated structure to the right. I descended a few steps, then, reaching an open doorway in the side of the building, entered and found myself at the top of a spiral staircase. I ran down the stairs until I found my progress blocked by a wooden door with rusty iron plates bolted to its surface.

The door opened after a few seconds, revealing a lumpy face with flat, bored-looking eyes set close together. I had seen such eyes before, in killer sharks off the Kenya coast. I took in the immaculately tailored grey uniform — not Hodden Grey but a charcoal colour — and the gold eagles embroidered on the shoulders. Beyond him I could see a small stone chamber with a curious slot in the floor. My stomach churned with horror at the sight of a bound figure, then a tide of such violent anger surged through me that for a moment I felt faint. I knew that I was about to kill in cold blood.

Murder must have shown in my eyes, for he gave me a strange look and tried to shut the door. But adrenalin in huge quantities was pumping into my bloodstream and I seemed to have the strength of ten as I gave the door a violent shove. He reeled back then made a grab for a carbine propped against the wall. But I was in after him like an avenging whirlwind and kicked it out of reach.

In the corner, tied to a chair, was Rachel. Her clothing was torn and filthy. Terrible raw, red, circular patches disfigured her legs and forearms. The eyes that stared at me were those of a terrified and pain-racked animal.

"It wasn't me — I swear it," he protested. But guilt was plain in his face and in his fear-cracked voice. My expression must have told him that trying to convince me was a lost cause, for he tried to dive past me for the gun. I was away ahead of him. My knee, with the full force of my body behind it, drove into his stomach. As he doubled up, a thin, continuous scream escaping from his mouth. My gauntleted fist smashed full into his face, and I felt bone crunch soggily beneath my knuckles.

He collapsed like a punctured balloon. I thought the fight, if such a massacre can be called a fight, was over. But there I made a bad mistake. As I drew back my boot to stave in his skull, with no more compunction that I would have trodden on a poisonous spider, he rolled away and with a convulsive, twisting movement was suddenly swaying on his feet. His hand flashed inside his tunic and re-appeared holding something; with a click a long blade sprouted from his fist. He came at me with astonishing speed, considering his injuries. But I had time to grab the carbine and as he lunged for my belly, snapped over the safety catch and squeezed off.

Like the jet from a hose striking a paper doll, the stream of bullets lifted him clean in the air and slammed him back against the wall. I kept my finger pressed hard against the trigger while a solid blast of lead shredded the jerking puppet before me. When the magazine finally clicked empty, the thing that collapsed on the floor was scarcely recognisable as human.

After the deafening racket of exploding carbine shells, the silence was palpable. I gagged at the stench of blood and cordite that filled the chamber. Fortunately all my bullets seemed to have gone home — in that confined space a ricochet would have zipped about like a hornet in a jam jar. As I cut Rachel's bonds I glimpsed massive iron grillework through the slot in the floor, and realised that we must be above the portcullis gate.

"Come on," I urged. "Time to go."

But she made no move, just sat in the chair staring in front of her with wide, glazed eyes. It was not the time to be gentle. I slapped her hard across the cheek with my open palm and shouted into her face.

The blankness faded from her eyes and she was suddenly sobbing in my arms. "Oh God, Nick — it's been like some terrible, evil nightmare. They've been trying to make me tell them things I didn't know. They used lighted cigarettes on me. They were going to start on my face today. Oh Nick," and she buried her face on my shoulder, while her arms tightened round me convulsively and her body shook with sobs.

She was broken, but not beyond mending. With love and care the woman I remembered would re-emerge from this disfigured semblance. But first we had to get out of the castle. Picking up the empty carbine, so that to any casual observer I would appear as an armed escort in charge of Rachel, I led her out and up the spiral staircase. Signalling her to wait in

the entrance, I stepped out onto the Lang Stairs to check that the coast
was clear.

It wasn't. A tall figure burst from the fog below, where the stairs disappeared in swirling whiteness. A mane of red hair — that cliff-like
forehead — and a single look that went through me at high voltage.

21

The Half Moon Bastion

"WAINWRIGHT!" he exclaimed in a strange, choked voice. I think he had realised, in a flash of insight, that I was the instrument of his hopes' destruction. With a roar of rage he bounded up the steps towards me, ignoring the fact that I was apparently armed. Dropping the useless carbine, I turned and, with the sudden access of adrenalin that always gives the hunted advantage at the start of the chase, raced up the steps ahead of him. There was no question of taking Rachel with me. That way, our capture would be a total certainty, whereas if I could elude Tam Linn we might still conceivably get away. I hoped she was rational enough to stay hidden in the entrance meanwhile.

I sprinted round the end of a huge Gothic pile, through a narrow opening into a courtyard enclosed by buildings. Opposite me was an open doorway into which I darted, to find myself in a vast, medieval-looking hall hung with weapons and armour. I looked wildly for an exit but there was none: I had run myself into a trap.

As I turned back towards the doorway Tam Linn burst through it. For a few moments we stared at each other and, as before at Derry Lodge, I realised with a shock almost of horror that I could put no name to the colour of his eyes.

Then deftly he plucked a huge, two-handed claymore from the wall and advanced towards me, holding the fearsome weapon aloft. I retreated step by step, knowing that if he boxed me in a corner I was done for; with the mighty reach of that terrible blade, he would cut me down like corn before the scythe if I tried to dodge past him.

With mounting despair I saw that he was herding me skilfully towards the far end of the great hall. I kept trying to work round to the side, in order to slip past him and gain the doorway, but always that enormously long blade would flicker out, to prevent me from outflanking him.

150

"Nick!"

I looked towards the doorway and there in the entrance was Rachel. As Tam Linn involuntarily turned his head in her direction, I dashed to the side.

Air fanned my cheek as the blade of the claymore whistled inches from my head.

Then I was past him and sprinting for the entrance. Grabbing a spear from a rack, Rachel tossed it to me as I came level with her. I caught it without breaking stride, skidded through the doorway and flew across the courtyard. As I darted through a gap between corner buildings, I heard Tam Linn's footfalls thudding yards behind me. Otherwise he made no sound.

A low, concave wall, pierced with embrasures for cannon, loomed before me through the fog. With a shock of dismay, I realised where we were — inside the ramparts on top of the Half Moon Bastion. Below was a sheer drop of a hundred feet or more. And behind me, guarding the open end of the Bastion's great semicircle, was Tam Linn. I was finally run to earth.

But as I turned to face him I was not entirely without hope. For in handing me a spear Rachel had provided me with the one weapon in that great hall that gave me something like a fighting chance against my adversary. In my Kenya boyhood my daily companion had been the son of my father's head herdsman, who had taught the two of us how to use a spear. Over endless hours I had mastered the smooth forward movement of the arm, and the final flip of the wrist which sent the missile spinning through the air with a force and accuracy that could spit a buck at twenty paces.

Now, as I hefted the spear in my hand, testing its balance, I felt muscle-memory returning to my arm. I reminded myself that I would have only the one chance. My chest tightened and I felt my mouth go dry.

Tam Linn halted about twenty yards from me. Clearly he thought my spear a trivial threat. With a grim smile of triumph he swung the great sword up in the air as though it were a stick and, whirling it round his head in a glittering arc, rushed upon me like a Highlander at Culloden.

My arm seemed almost to act of its own accord, raising and throwing the spear in a single, fast, flowing movement.

It took him full in the chest. The impact brought him to a sudden halt. The claymore flew from his hands and spun, ringing and clattering across the paving stones. Grasping the shaft as though to tug it free, he staggered past me, swaying, towards the rampart. At that moment a fog-wreath came curling through one of the gun-ports, enveloping his almost motionless figure. When it cleared, he had vanished.

I rushed to the spot and looked down. But the fog had swallowed up all sight and sound of him.

There is little more to tell. Basset, on receiving Palmer's message, had proceeded to withdraw south-east to the Moorfoot Hills and allowed the Republicans to deploy behind his old positions. Then he struck at them, smashing through their centre and surrounding the greater part of their force. Daft Davie, realising that he was in a hopeless military situation, had the good sense to surrender. A remnant of the part that had escaped encirclement would not give in, however, and retreated across Auchencorth Moss and through Penicuik Woods, fighting a stubborn rearguard action until brought to bay at Rullion Green below the Pentlands. Here, where more than three centuries before a Covenanting army had been destroyed, the remainder of the Republican force made a final stand — and were broken and scattered. On the following day Basset occupied the capital where, in the great Debating Chamber of the Parliament Buildings, the Wardens of the Council of the Scottish Republic made formal cession of their powers to the English Commander-in-Chief, as representative of Her Majesty's Government at Westminster.

Of Tam linn no trace was ever found. It is inconceivable to me that he could have survived either the spear wound or the fall from the Half-Moon Bastion; nevertheless one hears occasional rumours that he is in hiding in the Highlands, moving from village to village receiving the same native hospitality once accorded to a fugitive Stewart Prince.

If so, it will be no easy task for him to rally Scotland again. With Daft Davie Campbell and the other Republican leaders awaiting trial for High Treason and an English Army of Occupation policing the land, with the Chamber permanently dissolved, Scottish representation at Westminster ended, and the running of the country in the hands of a Minister for Northern Affairs, any attempt to regain independence might seem hopeless. The present situation could be likened to that which obtained in Scotland after the execution of William Wallace — that is, before Bruce came along to fan the embers into a blaze which all the world never dreamed of seeing again.